Barry Graham is a writer and performance artist and the author of three previous books and two chapbooks. His prose and poetry have appeared in several newspapers and magazines.

He was born in Glasgow in 1965 and has had a variety of occupations, including boxing and journalism. He has travelled widely and now lives in Edinburgh with his wife, American poet and fiction writer Marina Blake.

He is a serious student of Zen Buddhism and ethnopoetics. He appears regularly on TV and radio.

The Book of Man

BARRY GRAHAM

Library of Congress Catalog Card Number: 95-68387

A complete catalogue record for this book can be obtained from the British Library on request

The right of Barry Graham to be identified as the author of this work has been asserted by him in accordance with the Copyright, Designs and Patents Act 1988

Copyright © 1995 Barry Graham, God bless him

First published in 1995 by
Serpent's Tail, 4 Blackstock Mews, London N4, and 180 Varick Street, 10th floor, New York, NY 10014

Set in 10½pt Plantin by CentraCet Ltd, Cambridge
Printed in Great Britain by Cox & Wyman Ltd, Reading, Berks.

Foreword

Most of the places described in this book are real, but this is a work of fiction, and all characters and events are the product of my imagination.

I'm indebted to my friends for their kindness, support and encouragement, especially John McKenzie and Tom Kane. Nine bows.

Others who have helped inspire me and keep me sane are: Paul Reekie, Fjaere Nilssen, Frankie Mooney, Ken Wolverton, Tom McGrath, Tim Man, Mike Petty, John Hendrickse, Hal Sirowitz and Irvine Welsh.

Thanks to Anne Welsh, for a boost to my confidence just when I needed one.

And to Jade Reidy, whose poetry provided a key image for this book.

And I salute the memory of the composer Harry Partch, whose album *The World of Harry Partch* is the source of other images.

But all of the above pales into insignificance compared with the love, support and understanding I have had from my wife, Marina Blake. Without her, this book could not have been finished.

Barry Graham
New Year's Day 1994
Leith

for Marina
who walks on water
and gives me everything –

on we go.

The raven isn't evil,
it's just a black bird.

– Lucy Johnstone

May all who read this
get a lift right away

– graffiti on a bridge

One

Life, eh? That rich tapestry. That old black magic. This sodden existence.

from *The Book of Man* by Michael Illingworth

I ONLY WENT BACK out of curiosity. I don't want you thinking any of the crap some of my friends thought when I told them. It wasn't some hidden part of me that cared for them and drew me back. I never gave two fucks about them and I still don't. And I didn't go back on the rebound from my marriage breaking up – that'd happened five or six years before. I only went back out of curiosity, and it wasn't even curiosity that brought me back to Glasgow.

I arrived with just a big rucksack. In it were some clothes, toiletries and a copy of each of Mike's books. I got off my train about three in the afternoon. Glasgow Central Station didn't look like the same place where I'd got on a train to London ten years earlier. The floor was as polished as an ice-rink and there were potted plants everywhere. The noticeboards had been replaced with computer screens. There were still tramps begging at the station's entrance.

I walked up Renfield Street, which hadn't changed noticeably, and wondered what to do. It's strange arriving in a city when it's not a holiday and nobody's expecting you. During the day people are at work and in the evening everybody you go to see is doing something else and has to make the effort to fit you in.

There were some new bookshops. I drifted through them and was surprised to find Mike's books in all but one. Dying's a great career move.

I went along Sauchiehall Street to the Third Eye Centre. It was bigger than it had been, and it wasn't called the Third Eye Centre any more. But it was the same place. I thought of using the payphone to ring Floozy and check David was all right, but it'd just have gobbled up my change. I decided to wait till the evening when it'd be cheap rate.

I had a meal in the Third Eye's café. There was a poem on the wall, written for the place by a famous Glasgow poet. I read it after I'd eaten. By then it was six o'clock.

I made up my mind to go and see Paul first. He lived in Kersland Street, in the West End. I took the tube from St George's Cross to Hillhead and walked the five minutes' distance. I found Paul's close, climbed the stairs and found a door with his name and the names of three other people on it. I rang the bell and got no answer.

I found a pub with a TV at the bottom of Byres Road. I'd have a drink, watch Francine's show and then try Paul again.

The pub was quiet. I got a Southern Comfort and lemonade and decided to call Floozy. The London numbers in my address book seemed strange now. I dialled her number, prefixing it with 071, and got her answering machine.

"Hello. This is Floozy Thompson. I'm not in right now.

What a bummer, eh? Oh, well. The good Lord sends these things to try us. Leave a short, inspiring message and I'll call you right back." The theme from *Hawaii-Five-O* sounded briefly, then the bleep.

"Hi. It's Kevin. Just to let you know I got here in one piece. I'll ring you tomorrow. Hello to David." I hung up.

There was nearly an hour left before Francine's show came on, but I wasn't in a hurry. I finished my drink, got another and wondered why, after ten years away, it didn't seem strange. Maybe because, for the past four weeks, my thoughts had been back here.

Hearing of his death was strange, because I loved him. There are people in my life I've simultaneously loved and hated, but all I ever felt for him was unmitigated love. I hadn't spoken to him for about ten years.

I read about it in the *Guardian*. I'd bought the paper in the morning, but I was busy all day and didn't get a chance to read it until about midnight. I'd put David to bed, watched TV for a while and drunk some tea. I started to flick through the paper just to make having bought it worthwhile, and found the obituary.

Chronicler of Despair Dies

Michael Illingworth, the bleak writer from Glasgow, died of AIDS in one of the city's hospitals last week.
He was 35.
Illingworth became addicted to heroin while studying philosophy at Glasgow University. After being expelled, he wrote his first novel, the existential satire *Thus Spake Andy Schuster*. His best and most

> original work was the despairing novel *The Book of Man*, with its harrowing accounts of drug abuse and urban alienation. The book was banned from public libraries under legislation preventing local authorities from promoting homosexuality.
>
> Illingworth published only two books and was living in poverty during the last few years of his life.

I made some more tea and wondered how he'd got it. It could've been from sex or shooting up. One was as likely as the other, and I couldn't imagine him taking care with either.

I didn't feel like crying or anything, but I didn't want to go to bed. My small living room was cluttered with books and I had to search for a few minutes before I found *The Book of Man*. It was the hardback copy he'd given me just after it was published. His photo was on the dustjacket. I opened it and looked at the inscription on the flyleaf. *To Kevin Previn, with love and good wishes for the future – Mike Illingworth*. And the date.

I sat up all night in my chair in front of the gas fire, drinking tea and re-reading the book. It was very effective and very affected. Brilliant narration was interspersed with undergraduate, quasi-existential posing. He described a guy who'd go to pubs alone and sit down and pretend to himself that he was meeting someone there. That was wanky. It was also true and I thought of the man and it hurt.

Two

I was three or four when I discovered I was going to die. I used to look at the heads on pennies and ask my father whether the people were still alive. If he said they were dead, I'd ask what they'd died of and he'd say old age. Finally I asked him what old age meant and he explained to me that everybody dies eventually. I was aghast. "Will I die?" I asked him. He said yes, but not for a long time yet. I threw a tantrum, saying I didn't want to die. Then I forgot about it. Until the age of about eighteen, I thought there was going to be an exception made for me.

from *The Book of Man* by Michael Illingworth

I WATCHED FRANCINE'S show. This time she had the editor of a tabloid newspaper facing someone who was suing him for libel. It was tamer than it might've been. When it'd finished, I went back up to Paul's.

The walk up to Kersland Street took me ten minutes. It was dark and icy. I rang the doorbell and it was answered by a Tom Selleck lookalike. "Is Paul Keane here?"

"No. He's out."

"Any idea when he'll be back?"

"About an hour."

In fact, it was two and a half hours before Paul appeared. Tom Selleck, whose name turned out to be Neil, let me wait in the kitchen. He made me cups of tea and we chatted awkwardly. He'd assumed I was one of Paul's bum chums and seemed to become suspicious when it came up that I wasn't gay.

Paul arrived at midnight. He came into the kitchen, looked at Neil, looked at me and looked shocked. He just said, "Oh. It's you," and went to pour himself some tea.

"Hi," I said. "Did you get my letter?"

"Yeah."

Neil stood up. "I'll leave you to it," he said and went out.

Paul sat down on the chair where Neil had been. He was a tall, slender queen in his early thirties. He looked at me and said nothing.

"Sorry for just turning up like this," I said. "But I got no answer when I phoned."

"The phone's been knackered for months," he said. His accent was standard Central Scotland Queenspeak, high and mincing.

"I thought you'd have answered my letter," I said.

"I was going to. But I didn't feel like it. It took you long enough to get in touch with any of us."

I didn't say anything.

"How much are they paying you?"

"What?" I said, but I knew what he was talking about.

"The programme, dear. How much're you getting?"

"Not that much. And that's not why I'm doing it."

"I didn't see you at the funeral," he said.

"I didn't know when it was." *But I wouldn't have gone anyway*.

"Or at the hospital before he kicked it."

"I didn't know he was ill. There was nothing about it in the papers. The first I saw of it was the obituary in the *Guardian*."

"He was ill, all right."

"How long did he have it?"

"Don't know. He only found out once the symptoms started. That was about three or four months ago."

I looked at him. "Could you have it?"

"I could, but I don't. I had a test when I found out about Mike."

"Were you and him still shagging?"

"Fuck, no. We finished it years ago. I still gave him the odd hand-job, right enough."

A big white cat came into the kitchen and miaowed. "Haven't those bitches fed you, dear?" Paul asked it. It miaowed again. "Don't you worry. Your Auntie Paul'll look after you." He opened a tin of something and put it in the cat's dish on the floor.

"You should've seen him dying," he told me, sitting down again. "One time I took him some books. He wasn't sleeping at night – the skin cancer made him uncomfortable – and he liked to read. But the bulb in the reading lamp had conked out. He asked the nurse for another one. She said they didn't have another in the ward, but she'd go to another ward and try to borrow one. Off she went. Mike and I were laughing about it. But then she came back and said the other ward didn't have a bulb to spare. So Mike asked when he could have one, and she said he couldn't, the hospital had spent its budget for the year. Said it wasn't their fault, blame it on the NHS cuts. I brought him a bulb the next day – " Suddenly his voice quavered. "But can you believe that? The council spends forty fucking million on Glasgow being the European Cultural Capital, *and one of the best writers Glasgow's ever had rots away in the dark because there's no money to buy him a fucking lightbulb!*"

All at once he was crying, body shaking, hands over his face.

I got up and dragged my chair round to his side of the table and put my arms around him. "I *miss* him, Kevin," he whimpered against my shoulder.

I missed him too, but it'd have sounded stupid.

When I told Paul I hadn't arranged anywhere to spend the night, he said I could crash on a couch in the boxroom. It was more of a cupboard. Paul gave me a quilt and a pillow and a bottle of lice-killing lotion. "We've all had crabs lately," he told me. "Might still be in the bedding. Splash yourself down with this in the morning." I still don't know whether he was winding me up.

He said he had two other flatmates who wouldn't be back till about four in the morning. "I'll leave them a note saying you're here. You won't be buggered in your sleep."

There was no window in the room. When I turned the light off, I could see nothing except the figures on the digital clock. I'm long and thin and the couch was short and broad and I couldn't get comfortable. I thought about Mike.

He was great, and the obituary in the *Guardian* wasn't enough. A day or two after I'd read it, I wrote a clumsy tribute to him, an essay on him and his work. Nobody would publish it.

I ranted about it to Francine when we met for a drink. I had first met her because of Mike and she knew most of what had happened.

The day after I spoke to her, she rang me. "Just to

forewarn you," she said. "Channel Four want you to research and write a documentary about Mike Illingworth. Boucher, the producer, says he'll phone you soon."

He did. We talked about money, not much of it, and agreed. Then we talked about time. He wanted it written quickly, while it was still current. I told him I'd go to Glasgow the following week.

I wrote to a few people there. Some replied. David was a problem; I'd no intention of taking him with me. Peter and Francine would normally have taken him, but they were going on holiday. Then Floozy surprised me by offering to take him, and I astounded myself by saying okay.

Three

> This imbecility about love and destiny. There are any number of people you'd fall in love with if you met them. And when one love is taken away, you just fall in love with somebody else. Circumstantial, nothing else.
>
> from *The Book of Man* by Michael Illingworth

I DIDN'T SLEEP MUCH. I got up at eight and deloused myself with the lotion Paul'd given me. Then I dressed and went into the kitchen and helped myself to his tea bags. Outside the window, rain was coming down. Petrol and coffee smell, water and glass. A West End Saturday morning.

I was making more tea when Paul came in. He was barefoot and wore jeans and a T-shirt. "Give me a cup," he told me. "Milk and one sugar." He sat down at the table.

I poured two cups and put one down in front of him. "Thanks." He looked embarrassed. "Sorry about last night's display."

I sat opposite him. "Don't worry about it."

He drank some tea. "I'll make some breakfast when I've finished this."

"Thanks."

"You never said much about yourself last night," he said.

"You never asked."

"Are you still married?"

"No. I don't know if I'm divorced or widowed. Helene went back to Greece a few years ago. I haven't heard from her."

"Did she take the kid?"

"No. He's with me."

"What's his name again?"

"David."

"Oh, yeah. Right." He looked at me. "He's probably better off with you."

"I think so."

"Are you on your own, or have you got another woman?"

"Sort of. She doesn't live with me."

"Can't have been easy with David, then. Just you and him."

"It hasn't been. Still, being a single parent's got its problems, but it pulls girls like you wouldn't believe."

Paul laughed.

When she left, it was more of a disappointment than a heartbreak. It started as a romance and became an arrangement. I loved the idea of the house with the fire and the kids and someone to love me and even believe in me a bit, but it wasn't like that. It was dirty dishes and moods and sleeping with other people and jealousy and screaming at each other.

Paul made some porridge. "Was Mike still getting his stuff from Alfie?" I asked him.

"Yeah. Right up till he went into hospital."

"I'll want to talk to him. I wrote to him last week, but he didn't write back." I laughed. "Probably can't read."

"What address did you write to him at?"

"Allander Street."

Paul shook his head. "Fuck, you have been away. He

moved out of there a couple of years ago. Then he did a year in the Bar-L. He lives in Killearn Street now."

"What number?"

"Don't know. I haven't been up there. I haven't seen Alfie since I got off the junk myself."

"I'll find him," I said.

"He's supposed to be in a bad way with drugs himself these days."

"What, with smack? He never used to."

"Don't know if it's smack."

"What is it, then?"

"Don't know. I've only heard. But whatever it is, he's supposed to be shooting it."

"Sounds a lovely scene."

"I've heard it's pretty. It's not just junk and muscle he's into these days. He's got a wife now, and he's put her and her sister on the game."

"Great thing, free enterprise."

I left and walked up to Possil.

I met Mike and Helene on the same night and in the same place. It was a Saturday, and I'd been taken along and signed into Strathclyde University's Students' Union by a girl who'd deserted me during the disco. I sat at the bar morosely downing snakebites, then went outside for a drunken wander up and down the stairs of the building. When I went back to the disco, the bouncer said I was too drunk and wouldn't let me in.

Drunk I was, but I planned to get drunker. I went downstairs to the alternative disco, where they'd let anybody in, even me. The music was mostly Goth, but I wasn't there to dance. I went straight to the bar and ordered a pint of snakebite.

Time went by. I stopped feeling depressed and started feeling philosophical, though I couldn't remember how to spell it. I watched the Goths in their black gear and wondered if they could see the rest of their lives coming and were in mourning because of it.

Then the contents of my stomach gave me a nudge to let me know they were coming up and wasting no time about it. Swallowing it down, I lurched over to the door, out of the disco, and ran full pelt along the corridor to the toilets.

I don't know if the cubicles in the men's bogs at Strathclyde Union have locks that work nowadays, but I can testify that they didn't use to. I pushed a cubicle door, it opened and I bade a fast farewell to a gutful of snakebite. My eyes watered from the force of it, and it was a few seconds before I realised I'd vomited all over a guy who was sitting on the throne, trousers around his ankles, quietly having a crap.

He said something that didn't sound like "Thank you". In the logic of drunken panic, I was suddenly aware of two things. 1) If somebody puked on me like that, I'd belt him. 2) If he attacked me in my present state, I wouldn't stand a chance.

So I'd better get him first. I hauled off and hit him in the face with as good a right hand as I could muster under the circumstances and got out of there.

A sensible man would have gone home. So I went back to the alternative disco. I drank some fresh orange juice and lemonade. My stomach kept threatening to throw it back up, but I made it stay down and had some more.

By the time the disco closed and they were chucking everybody out, I wasn't any more sober. But I wasn't any worse and I'd got hold of myself enough to walk straight. I joined the crowd of patrons of both discos out on the stairway. And heard somebody say, "*That's him! That's him there!*" And I was grabbed by a bouncer and the guy I'd shared the toilet with.

I pleaded guilty and tried to explain. The bouncer asked my victim if he wanted the police called. He said no.

"Fuck off," the bouncer told me. "You're barred. I'll remember your face – and if you ever come back here I'll rearrange it."

Outside, I stood taking big breaths of cold night air and being glad to be in one piece. Then I was surrounded by the guy from the bog and about a dozen others, some of them girls.

"Tell me something," he said to me. He was short and squat but looked horribly agile, like a monkey. There was a cut on his cheek where I'd hit him, but he looked like he could take care of me easily if it came down to it. "You were drunk. Fair enough. You had to be sick in a hurry. Very good. The lavvy doors don't lock. Excellent. You didn't know I was there till you puked on me. Wonderful. *But what the fuck did you hit me for?*"

"'Cause I thought you'd belt me one for puking on you," I said dazedly.

His friends were laughing and so was he. "Fuck's sake," he said. "Listen. We're going to a party. You can come too, if you promise not to hit anybody. You can puke on them if you like."

I went. The party was in a flat at Cowcaddens, about fifteen minutes' walk. On the way, the guy said his name was Mike. I told him my name and apologised for the puke and the punch.

"Don't worry about it."

"Your jumper's in quite a state," I said. "Sorry."

"Don't worry about it," he said again.

The party was on its last legs when we arrived. There wasn't much booze left, but I'd had about as much as I could handle anyway. Mike went off to take a shower. I sat on the floor with his friends, awkwardly sipping water from a pint glass and listening to whatever was coming out of the hi-fi.

His friends had mostly split into groups and it was a few minutes before anybody spoke to me. Finally a girl with fair hair and strangely dark skin asked me, "What's your name?"

"Kevin. What's yours?"

"Helene."

"Helen?"

"No. Helene. It's Greek."

"Are you Greek?"

"Yeah. Are you?"

"No," I said. Neither was her accent. "You sound Scottish."

"I came here when I was two. Are you a student?"

"Yeah. Are you?"

"No. At Strathclyde?"

"No," I said. "Somebody signed me in tonight. I'm at Langside College."

"What're you doing?"

"Just a couple of Highers."

"I just got signed in tonight as well," she said. "By Mike."

"Is he your boyfriend?" I don't beat around the bush when I'm out of my face.

"No. He's my friend's boyfriend."

"Oh." Pause. "What do you do?"

"I'm in the Three Million Club. Have been since I left school."

"When was that?"

"Five years ago. I'm twenty-three."

"Same age as me."

She took a gulp from a glass of something amber. "Haven't you got a drink?" she asked.

"Yeah." I held up my glass.

"What is it?"

"Water."

"Awww. Have some of this."

I shook my head. "Nah. I've had enough. And I shared most of it with Mike."

Helene laughed. "Yeah. Nobody'd believe him when he came into the disco with his face cut and sick dripping off him. He said, 'I've heard nothing happens without a reason. Okay. I was in the lavvy having a shit, and this fucking sociopath came in, puked on me, punched me and ran away. Anybody got a theory as to *why*?'"

"He's been good about it," I said.

"Yeah. That's what he's like. I think he was only pissed off 'cause you hit him. I don't think he minded the sick."

"What's he do? I take it he's a student?"

"Yeah, but not at Strathclyde. He's doing philosophy at Glasgow Uni. But I think he's going to quit."

"How come?"

"He doesn't like it. He's in trouble for not going to lectures. He's supposed to have been writing a book instead."

"How d'you mean, supposed to?"

"Well, nobody's seen it."

I steered the conversation back to her and we swapped biographies for a while. Then I said, "Mike's taking his time over that shower."

"Probably taking a fix as well," she said.

Four

I was waiting to score and he was late as usual. I was lucky this time, though. I'd just fixed up and I wasn't in a hurry. I went into a chip shop and got something to eat. A Tracy or Sharn from the schemes served me. She demands your order in a schemie accent, and glowers at you as she gets it. It's not just that she hates you, though she probably does. It's the existence she endures, sweating in that chip shop and then going home to Easterhouse or whatever scheme she's from to listen to Radio One and be fucked by some poor drongo who can't do any better. And she'll always live that way, because she's got no way out of it. Though she's miserable, she doesn't know why. She's unhappy because she's too stupid to get out of it, but too stupid to know that's why she's unhappy.

from *The Book of Man* by Michael Illingworth

POSSIL'D HARDLY changed at all in ten years. They'd closed down the Askit factory, knocked down a couple of buildings and opened a supermarket. The bad end of Killearn Street was exactly as I remembered it. It was still raining.

I stopped an old man wearing a bunnet. "Any idea what number Alfie Birrel stays at?" I asked him.

He knew and he told me.

I found the close and climbed the stairs. The flat was on

the top floor. The name *Birrel* was scrawled on a piece of paper sellotaped to the door. There was no doorbell. I knocked.

No answer.

I knocked again, and heard what sounded like a gunshot from inside. I thought of heading back down the stairs. I knocked again, hard, and realised the door was open. I pushed it open further and went in.

There was nobody in the hall and it was completely bare. Not a carpet on the floor. The walls were burnt in places. I heard another gunshot from one of the rooms. I knocked loudly on the door.

"*Whut is it?*"

I opened the door and went in. "How're you doing, Alfie? Remember me?" I said, knowing that he would.

"Jesus fuck. Kevin Previn." He was a massively built man in his early forties. He wore jeans and a filthy T-shirt and held an air rifle. There was a boy of about eight with him.

"That's my name," I said. I went over to him and held out my hand. He shook it.

"Howyi doin, mate?"

"All right. I'm up to see about Mike."

He gestured with the rifle. "Oot the wiy."

I moved beside him and he started shooting again. He'd drawn a target – a man's head and body – on the wall. It was riddled with pellet-marks, and the floor was dusty with plaster.

"Wherryi livin' noo?" he asked me.

"London. Been there for ten years."

"Aye. Ah kin hear it in yur voice."

"Fuck. Everybody down there thinks I've got a Glasgow accent."

"Yi huv. But yi sound like a poof noo."

I didn't rise to it. "Very nice," I said, as he fired a pellet into the middle of the target's forehead.

"How kin we no' shoot the windies across the road?" the kid said.

"'Cause Ah fuckin' sayed so, that's how."

"Even Alfie doesn't do that," I said.

"Aye he does," the kid said.

"He knows his da," Alfie said, laughing.

I was surprised. "What, he's yours?"

"Aye. Whose d'yi think?"

"I've got one myself."

"Ah know," he said, and I remembered he did.

"What're you up to these days? Still dealing?"

"Aye. An' sortin' cunts noo an' again."

I thought of asking if he was taking junk himself, and decided against it. He wasn't a difficult guy to provoke.

"So whut is it aboot Mike?" he asked me.

"I'm doing a programme about him for TV. A documentary."

"Ah'm gaun on nae fuckin' telly."

"You don't have to. I just want to find out what was going on with him before he died. I'm just talking to people who knew him. Some of them'll be on the programme, but you don't have to."

I could just imagine the programme if Alfie was on it: interviews with Paul and others, their names and connections with Mike appearing on the screen, then Alfie's glowering face and the title *Alfie Birrel – his pusher*.

"No' much Ah kin tell yi," he said. He put down the rifle. "He joost came tae get his gear. Ush'lly sat an' blethered fur a while. C'moan tae the livin' room." He turned and went out of the room with the kid in tow. I followed.

The living room had no carpets and was furnished only with a decrepit three-piece suite, a gas fire and a cooker. On the couch, covered by a quilt, lay a sick-looking blonde woman in her twenties. "She's goat hepatitis," Alfie said by way of introduction. I said hello to her and she said nothing.

I sat in one of the armchairs and Alfie sat in the other. "How d'you think he got it?" I asked.

"Goat whut?"

"AIDS. Did he share his works?"

"Don't know. Don't think so. He jacked up here a coupla times. Alwis had his ain works."

"Did you go and see him in hospital?" I already knew the answer.

"Naw. Didny know he wis in at furst. He joost stoapped comin'. Ah thoat mibbe he wis tryin' tae come aff it. Ah only heard aboot a week 'fore he died."

"Did he ever talk about wanting to come off?"

"Fuck, naw. But Ah didny really know the cunt. We nivur talked aboot things like that. We joost blethered. He wis a good wee cunt."

"Alfie, get that wean," the woman on the couch said tiredly. The kid was stealthily opening the door, trying to sneak out.

"C'mere, ya wee cunt!" Alfie went after him, caught him, and they wrestled on the floor, laughing and swearing at each other.

"*Alfie, stoap it! Stoap the fuckin' kerry-oan!*" the woman said. He did stop it, cuffing the kid and telling him to sit where he was and keep his fucking gub shut. The woman lay with her eyes closed. "Ah'm fuckin' sickythis," she said.

"Fuckin' sick uptyhere." She didn't specify where. "Ah'll neety jack up."

"So wull Ah," said Alfie.

"I didn't think you'd take the stuff yourself," I told him.

"It's no' smack. It's pills," he said.

I watched as he got his works out, crushed up the pills and filled the syringe. "Me furst," the woman said. He handed it to her, but she couldn't do it. "Canny find a vein. Ma haunds're shakin' too much."

"So wull mine be," Alfie said.

I stood up. "I'll do it." I went over and knelt by the couch.

"D'you know how?" said the woman.

"Yeah. I've done it before."

She handed me the works. I looked at her arm. There were white lines where most of the veins had collapsed, but a couple were still useable. "Have you got a tourney?" I asked Alfie.

"Use yur belt," he said.

I took off my belt and fastened it round her arm, then pulled tight. The veins stood out, and I pressed the needle in. I put the stuff in her, then withdrew the needle.

"Ta," she said as it hit her.

"Gie's it," said Alfie.

"If she's got hepatitis, you'd better sterilise this before you use it," I said.

"Aye, Ah know."

I helped him fix as well and left soon after. He hadn't really been able to tell me anything about Mike, but I hadn't expected him to. I'd just wanted to have another look at the scene.

It was still raining. I walked along the road to the supermarket. I wouldn't have thought there'd ever be a supermarket in Possil. I went in and walked around. It was quite something. The only supermarket I've ever been in where every third customer's walking around with a dog. There was a delicatessen that sold only grapes and Scottish Cheddar, and the two women behind the counter were smoking.

I imagined Mike walking round the place with me. I remembered a time, not long before I last saw him, when I'd visited him in the West End, where he'd a flat. He was lying on his bed, just having taken a fix. He seemed distant and depressed, and I asked why.

He gazed at the ceiling as he spoke. "Cunts don't know what the fuck's going on. Academic arseholes sitting at their word processors, writing their books, or books about books, and feeling so important. Whatever you write, you preach to the converted. You don't make any difference to the pie-and-chips-and-fish-suppers belt, Possil and Easterhouse and Maryhill. They're all dropping with cancer and fuck knows what. What difference is *The Book of Man* going to make to anybody?"

I left the supermarket and went to the safer end of Killearn Street, where Helene and I lived for a while. The close had an entryphone now. Apart from that it was still the same.

The day after I'd met Mike, I phoned him. It was three o'clock on a Sunday afternoon, and I woke him.

"Illingworth's Early Morning Telephone Friends Ltd," he said when he finally answered the phone.

"It's not early morning. It's Kevin here, Mike. Remember me?"

"Kevin of the iron fist and cider-scented puke? I'll have a hard job forgetting."

I laughed. "Did I wake you up?"

"Yeah."

"Sorry. I was just calling to see if you fancied meeting up."

I heard him yawn. "Oh, yeah. Yeah." A slurping noise. "Pardon my orange juice." More slurping. "Yeah. Tell you what – are you up to anything tonight?"

"No."

"Why don't you come over here, then? We can take it from there."

"Where's here?"

"Didn't I tell you?"

"No. Just gave me your phone number."

"Oh. I'm at 41 Otago Street. At Kelvinbridge."

"Yeah. I know it."

"Whereabouts're you?"

"St George's Cross." Only about ten minutes' walk from his place. "What time should I come over?"

"Soon as you like," he said.

I went over about an hour later. It was a spacious, self-contained bedsit, reasonably furnished and with its own cooker and shower. The phone was in the hall, just outside his door. There were two chairs in front of a small electric fire. Mike and I sat in them, facing each other. He wore baggy cords and a big seaman's jumper. He was barefoot. The left side of his face was swollen from the punch I'd given him.

I looked at it and made a face. "Fuck. I didn't realise it was that bad."

He laughed. "It doesn't hurt. I expected a headache, but I think I've slept it off."

"I hear you've been writing a book," I said as he poured some tea.

"Who told you?"

"Helene."

He nodded. "Yeah. It seems to be doing the rounds. I wanted it kept quiet. But I told that bitch Moira, and she told everybody else."

"Who's Moira?"

"My girlfriend. Or rather, she is till I give her the heave tomorrow. I'd do it tonight, but I'm in too good a mood to speak to her."

"Yeah, Helene said you were going out with a friend of hers."

"Not for much longer. But you must've seen her at the party. Kept cuddling me. Face like an armpit."

"Don't recall her. But I don't remember very much towards the end. Why's your book a secret?"

"It doesn't have to be, now that it's nearly finished. But when I started it, I wasn't sure I'd finish it. So I wasn't going to tell anybody."

"What's it about?"

He smiled. "The philosophy department at Glasgow Uni. It's called *Thus Spake Andy Schuster*."

I hadn't read much at that time and didn't get the joke of the title. "D'you think you'll get it published?"

"I fucking hope so. It's getting me kicked out of uni."

"How come?"

"I've hardly been to a lecture in months. So last week they got me up in front of the Board of Studies. Told me to explain my absence. I said, 'I've been writing a book.' They said, 'Don't you think your studies're more important?' They asked if I was going to apply myself in future. I said,

'I doubt it. I've got an idea for another book, so I expect I'll be writing that once I get this one finished.' I'm expecting the expulsion letter any day now."

"What'll you do?"

"I'm not bothered," he said. "I was planning to leave anyway. I only went to uni in the first place to please my folks."

"What made you pick philosophy?"

"Sounded like the best skive. I imagined the exam papers having questions like, *What is the meaning of life?* I didn't realise I'd have to read so many boring books."

Mike poured some more tea. "So what'll you do when they kick you out?" I asked him again.

"Don't know. The Lord will provide. I'm hoping this book'll get published and I can get on with another one. Or maybe I'll do some journalism or something."

"Couldn't you change to another course?"

"Probably. If I wanted to. But I don't."

"I thought of going to uni myself, when I finish doing these Highers. But I don't think I'll bother. I've had enough of being around academics."

He nodded. "Uni's even worse. They wouldn't know real life if it buggered them in broad daylight. But didn't you get any Highers at school?"

"Nah, I just pissed about. Failed my O-Grades and got kicked out when I was sixteen." *And the rest?*

"Yeah. You said something about that last night."

"I don't remember. But I don't remember much about the last part. I shouldn't have let Helene force that lager on me." I hesitated. "Did I happen to tell you anything in confidence last night?"

He smiled. "That you fancy Helene? Nah, you never said a word."

"Bastard." I laughed. "Don't say anything."

"Safe with me. So are you seeing her again?"

"I hope so. I don't know. I gave her my phone number, but I never got hers."

"Why not? Wouldn't she give you it?"

"Don't know. Can't remember."

He laughed again. "I'll get it off Moira."

"Thanks. I can't even remember if I asked her for it. I've had more blackouts lately than the Blitz."

Mike rubbed his swollen face. "Are you always like that with a drink in you?"

"No. I don't go around attacking people. And normally I don't drink much."

"Last night must've been pretty fucking abnormal, then."

"Well. I've been drinking a lot just lately."

"Any reason?"

"Not really. I've been a bit down, but there's no reason why. I've just felt like going out and throwing stones at cars or something."

He nodded. "I know the feeling."

"I was really pissed off last night. I was with a girl and she went off and left me. So I just got arseholed."

"I don't drink much myself," he said. I knew. Helene'd told me. "So – d'you think you and Helene'll soon be making the beast with two backs?"

I shrugged. "Do you?"

"No idea," he said. "I don't know her that well. But you might be in there. She's got funny tastes."

"Thanks."

He looked at me for a moment, considering, then said, "D'you mind if I take a fix?"

Helene'd told me about that as well. I'd been more intrigued than shocked. Now I was fascinated.

"No," I said. "Not at all."

He looked at me again, but didn't do anything. Then he went to a cupboard, got his stuff and began preparing it, cooking it in a spoon over the gas ring.

"What is it?" I asked him. "Heroin?"

"Yeah."

Watching someone fix is like watching someone wank. When the junk was ready and the syringe was full, he sat in his chair and rolled up the left sleeve of his jumper. He bound an old Paisley-patterned tie round his arm to make the veins stand out. Then he injected himself near the elbow. He kept the needle in for a while, letting a red ribbon of blood flutter into the syringe. Finally he pressed the plunger and pulled the needle out. He sat back and closed his eyes. His arm was bleeding but he didn't notice.

"Yes," he said.

That was all he said for a while. I didn't say anything. He sat there with his eyes closed and I sat opposite and watched him. I wondered if he was putting on a show for me.

When he opened his eyes, he looked at me and said, "Want to go out?"

"Where?"

"For a walk."

"All right."

The blood on his arm had dried. He rolled his sleeve down over it. "Come on, then." He put on shoes and socks and took a leather coat from a peg on the door. I put on my jacket.

*

"You should be careful who you do that in front of," I told him. We were walking towards Kelvingrove Park. He didn't answer. "You don't want somebody telling the police."

He looked at me with strange eyes. "Are you going to tell the police?"

"No."

"I didn't think so."

We entered the park. It was grey and cold.

"How long've you been on it?" I asked.

"A while."

"Are you hooked?"

"There's not much point otherwise."

Five

> If there's no God, then life is hopeless. If there is a
> God, considering what he allows to go on, life is
> really hopeless. Life is only varying degrees of
> suffering.
>
> from *The Book of Man* by Michael Illingworth

IT'S STRANGE WHEN you expect to feel strange and don't. Like when you go back to a place where – a long time ago – something important happened to you, and you feel no enormity or awe.

I'd been sitting on the steps of a close in Otago Street for nearly an hour, looking up at the window of the room Mike had lived in when we first met. I felt almost cheated because I'd expected to feel overcome and didn't.

It was getting cold. I walked around for a while. I couldn't think of anything else I could do at that time – it was early evening – and I didn't want to go back to Paul's yet. I didn't like him much and he didn't like me at all, which made it good of him to put me up.

I went into a pub in Great Western Road and got a Southern Comfort and lemonade. I sat at a table and drank it and thought about the people I should start trying to track down the next day.

There was a girl sitting at a table on the other side of the room. She had bobbed black hair. She wore jeans and a polo-neck and a miserable expression. She kept looking at her watch and looking ready to cry.

Then this guy came into the pub and her face came alive. She grinned at him as he sat next to her, and they kissed for a while. I heard him say he was sorry for being late. She laughed and said she hadn't been worried. They kissed some more.

I started thinking about Floozy. Up till then, I'd almost managed not to. I drank some more – I forget how much – but it didn't help. I laugh when I hear people talk about drinking to forget; for me, it brings the worst details back in technicolour.

I went to the payphone and called Floozy.

"H'lo?" Her voice was rough, husky. Thirty a day and plenty of spirits does that.

"Hi. It's Kevin."

"Oh. Hi."

"How're you doing with David?"

"Fine. Did you know he likes vodka on his cereal?"

"You're kidding. I hope."

"Yeah." She laughed. "David's fine. We're doing fine. Getting on great."

"Good."

"How's it going up there?"

"Okay. I've talked to a couple of people. I'll get hold of some more tomorrow."

"You feeling okay?"

"Yeah," I said. "Why?"

"You sound a bit down."

There's a surprise. "No more than I was."

"I'll have to get off," she said. "I'm in the middle of cooking pasta. And I'm expecting a call about a gig."

"Okay. Tell David I'll see him soon."
"D'you want to talk to him?"
"Nah. Better not. I've been drinking."
"Thought so. Phone tomorrow, will you?"
"Yeah."
"Take care of yourself."
"Love you."
"Take care. 'Bye."

I didn't feel like another drink. I left the pub and walked back to Paul's. There was a sticky drizzle. As I passed Hillhead Underground Station, I saw a guy busking just inside the entrance. There was hardly anybody about, but he carried on playing anyway. I knew how he felt.

I put some change in his guitar case and headed up Kersland Street. "How'd it go?" Paul asked as he let me in. "Did you find him all right?"

"Yeah. He couldn't tell me anything. Except that Mike took drugs. Bet you didn't know that."

He laughed sourly. "Was he surprised to see you?"

"Not very, or he didn't show it. Recognised me as soon as I walked in the door."

We sat in the kitchen. "I found something today," Paul told me. "Something you might remember."

It was a copy of the *Glasgow Herald* from twelve years ago. It had a photo of Mike and me at a reading we'd done at the Edinburgh Festival Fringe.

The caption read: *Controversial novelist Michael Illingworth with Kevin Previn, Glasgow's underground poet, playwright and songwriter.*

*

It was at a later Edinburgh Festival that I last saw Mike, about a year ago. He didn't see me.

I'd come up with Floozy to appear at a Fringe cabaret. The first night went well. Afterwards, we went back to somebody's flat and sat up all night, drinking and gloating. In the morning, Floozy and I were walking along Princes Street, still drunk, holding hands. We were looking for somewhere to have breakfast.

I saw a short, Neanderthal figure just ahead of us, standing at a traffic crossing. It was Mike Illingworth.

I could barely believe my tired eyes. I stood looking, not sure whether to go and speak to him. Then the light changed and he crossed the road.

I didn't see Mike again.

I still smelled of the stuff Paul'd given me to delouse myself. I had a shower and felt better. Paul asked if I wanted to stay another night. I said I'd arranged to stay somewhere else, which wasn't true. I knew Paul didn't believe me, but he was glad of the lie.

As I was leaving, Paul said, "Remember what you used to say about him? About him being a genius – ?"

I remembered. "Yeah. When he writes, he's a genius. When he thinks, he's a crank."

Paul nodded. "Are you going to say that in your programme?"

"Probably."

"Just say he was a little bent writer. Because that's all he was."

I thanked him for putting me up and went down the stairs and out into the frozen dark.

I found a bed and breakfast in Great Western Road and booked in. I didn't plan to stay there if I could find somebody else to crash with. I couldn't afford it. There wasn't much left of the commissioning fee I'd got from Channel Four. I'd used most of it to bring my mortgage up to date. I still had an overdraft that haunted me.

The room was all right. I went to bed and read some of *The Book of Man* before I slept.

Six

You know you're lonely – if you really need evidence – when you go for a drink with somebody you've nothing to say to, just to avoid staying in or sitting in the pub alone and stared at.

from *The Book of Man* by Michael Illingworth

I WOKE UP wanting to do nothing. I had tea and rolls for breakfast and looked through my notebook, reading the list of names and numbers I didn't want to call. It'd be nice to just go out and wander around the city and remember.

I used the payphone in the hall to call eight numbers. Five of them just rang, and the three that answered told me to call back in the late afternoon.

I spent the morning walking about in Kelvingrove Park, eventually crossing the bridge into the Maryhill side of the park, where I used to play when I was a kid. It didn't look like the same place. When I was eight, the park was totally wild. Walls were falling down or had fallen down already and the grass and trees were so unkempt as to make it a jungle – and a great place to play if you were eight years old and watched a lot of Tarzan films.

Now it was as elegant as the best Edinburgh park. The walls had been rebuilt, the grass had been cut and the bushes trimmed. I couldn't make any connection in my memory and I briefly thought I'd lost my way and found the wrong park. But you don't lose your bearings that easily, even after ten years.

I walked up the road out of the park we used to call the Low Road, the road that went past the army barracks and led to Raeberry Street, where I was born.

There was a tiny ledge jutting out from the bridge over the road, about forty feet high. When I was a kid, I used to spend hours sitting on that ledge with my best mate, Peter O'Connor. We'd sit with our legs dangling, right at the edge of that drop, and think nothing of it. Now the thought of that height terrifies me, and I'd be terrified for David if he went near it. Yet back then falling off wasn't even an issue. It couldn't happen. And it never did.

I'm only thirty-five. I'm too young to be scared.

I thought about climbing on to the ledge and sitting for a while with my legs dangling. But the thought was enough.

I walked back through the park. It'd crossed my mind to follow the Low Road up to Raeberry Street and see what'd changed, but I wasn't sure I ought to. And now definitely wasn't the time.

I crossed Byres Road, went along Bank Street and re-entered the park, coming out on to Sauchiehall Street on the other side. I thought about having lunch in the Centre for Contemporary Arts – which was the new name for the Third Eye Centre – but the memories were already coming at me too hard.

I found a greasy spoon in a sidestreet and ordered cheese omelette and chips with a mug of tea.

I was the only customer. The waitress and only visible member of staff was a middle-aged Italian woman. She looked bored, and sat smoking a cigarette after she served me.

The food wasn't as foul as it might've been. Getting back to my roots, I smothered it with tomato ketchup. While I was eating, another customer came in. He was in his twenties, with tattooed fingers, an undernourished moustache and a brown cord jacket. I'd never seen him before, but I recognised something.

The woman took one look at him and said, "Get out. I'm no' servin' you. Get out. There's a shop along the road. I'm no' servin' you."

He walked towards her. "But missus. Ah'm awright noo. Ah've been in rehab."

I knew it.

"I'm no' *servin*' you," she said again. "I'd enough trouble off you the last time."

"Gonnae joost gie's a hamburgur tae take away?" His voice was an aggressive wheedle.

"Go right now, or I'm phoning the police," she said.

"Fur fuck's sake!" The guy looked round in a fury, looking at me. I looked back at him, then looked away. "Ah only waant a fuckin' burgur – "

A jaundiced-looking woman stuck her head in the door. "Dodey, lea' it. C'm oan."

Dodey left, beaten. "Ah'm gonnae phone the Health Board," he called over his shoulder. "Ah saw a moose in yur back shoap."

The woman went over and pushed the door shut behind him. Then she turned and looked at me. "Drug addict," she said.

The day after I first saw Mike take a fix was Monday. I was at college in the morning and spent most of the afternoon in the library. When I got home, there was a note from one of my flatmates stuck to my bedroom door.

> *Mike called (noon).*
> *And again (3 pm).*

I made some tea and called him. "Kevin here. I heard you rang."

"Yeah. Just to give you Helene's number if you want it. I got it from Moira like I said."

"Great. Did you finish with Moira?"

"Uh-huh. Gave her the heave this morning when she phoned me. She wasn't pleased." He laughed. "Probably thinks I fancy Helene."

"I'll give her a ring. Will she be in now?"

"No reason why she shouldn't be. She's not working."

"Wait till I get a pen." I got one and he gave me the number. "Thanks. She'll probably tell me to fuck off."

"Don't know. Her last boyfriend was a wanker."

"I'm in with a chance, then."

"If you're not doing anything tonight, come round if you like," he said.

I phoned Helene.

"Hi, it's Kevin. We met at – "

"Yeah, I remember. Been sick on anybody since?"

I sighed. "This one's going to run and run."

She laughed. "How'd you get my number?"

"From Mike."

"He must've got it from Moira."

"Yeah. He did." I wondered if she knew they'd finished. "The reason I phoned – " *Go on, Kev. Dig in.* "I was wondering if you'd like to meet up for a drink. Or something. Sometime."

She laughed again. "Were you?" *That's it. Make it easy for me.* "Yeah, okay. When?"

"Whenever you like."

"Can't be tonight."

"How about tomorrow?"

"Can't. I'm skint."

"I'm not." My grant had come that very day. "How about tomorrow?"

Pause. Reluctantly, "Yeah, okay. If you're sure you don't mind."

"Right. Whereabouts?"

"I don't mind."

I considered. "D'you know the Arlington?"

"No."

"In Woodlands Road."

"Oh, yeah. I'll find it."

We said we'd meet at eight. Later that night, I went to see Mike. He wore a green fez and his eyes seemed tiny. "I've just been taking some stuff," he said as he let me in.

"Well, I rang Helene and – "

He cut me off. "Sit down. I'll be with you in a minute. He knelt on the floor, where a copy of the *Guardian* was spread out.

He took more than a minute; I watched as he turned the pages, reading every word on every page – including the classified ads.

Later, we talked a lot. He read to me from *Thus Spake Andy Schuster*. I wondered whether I dared show him some of my stuff.

*

"I think Mike's mad," I told Helene the next night.

She laughed and nodded. "It doesn't take people long to realise." We were sitting in the Arlington, a quiet old people's pub in the West End. "What'd he do?"

"When I arrived, he read a paper cover to cover. Says he does that a lot when he's had a fix. Then he got a pair of scissors and started cutting up the paper. I asked him what he was doing, and he said that if you cut up the headlines and mix them together, you sometimes get next week's headlines . . ."

Helene had a convulsion.

"I don't know if he was just winding me up," I said. "But he seemed serious. He seemed to believe it. I asked him how he knew, and he said he's always known."

She stopped laughing long enough to say, "I hadn't heard about that one, but it's typical – " And creased up again.

"He showed me some of his book," I said. "Read it to me."

She stopped laughing. "So it exists."

"It exists all right."

"What's it like?"

"The bits he read me are good. One bit's brilliant. I reckon when he writes, he's a genius. When he thinks, he's a crank."

She laughed again. "Better not tell him that. You're the only person he's shown the book to."

"Yeah. He seems to like me. I like him."

"So do I, but I wish I didn't. He's been really rotten to Moira."

"How?" She obviously didn't know they'd finished.

"Lots of things." She shrugged. "I don't want to repeat

things Moira's told me in confidence. But, for one thing, he fucks around a lot."

"Oh."

"And – speaking of fucking – "

I looked at her.

"I'll have another fucking drink," she said.

She was made for something much better than she got. I don't know whether she settled for so much less through choice, or because she felt she had to.

Now, with no way of getting in touch with her, or even knowing whether she's alive, the memories are strange. Going to the Edinburgh Festival. Walking around Glasgow's West End, holding hands and looking in shop windows. I'm not saying I miss her. It's just strange.

Seven

> If I can find a friend. A real one. I get so tired. People lean on me, but they won't let me lean on them. If there was somebody who'd love me and take me for myself. I think that's all I'd need.
>
> from *The Book of Man* by Michael Illingworth

I PHONED MY list of numbers again, late in the afternoon. They were all prepared to see me that evening. I arranged to meet two of them, each at a different time.

The first was Moira. I met her in the Atholl Bar in Renfrew Street at six.

It was a popular, central bar, frequented by a mixture of drama student posers and office types. I went in and wandered around, trying to spot someone who might be Moira. Eventually she had to call to me.

She was standing at the bar. "You haven't changed a bit," she said as I stood next to her. She had.

"Couldn't see you for the crowd," I said. I didn't want to tell her she was so eroded I didn't know her. "Want a drink?"

"I'll get it. I was just trying to get served. What d'you want?"

"Southern Comfort and lemonade."

She got the drinks and we went and sat at a table. "What're you up to these days?" I asked her.

"Teaching. Primary school."

"Married?"

"Divorced. You still with Helene?"

"No."

"What're you doing? D'you still write poetry?"

"Yeah. And plays. I do some editing for publishers, and some gigs." Pause. "Did you see anything of Mike?"

"Not really. Not deliberately. We never became friends again. We'd talk to each other when we met in the street. That happened a few times. You know how that is – Glasgow's a village."

"Yeah, I do know." There were people I'd been scared of meeting since I'd arrived.

"I knew he was ill, but I didn't know it was AIDS. I didn't go and see him in hospital," she said.

"Did you go to the funeral?"

She nodded. "So did a lot of people. There was quite a crowd."

"Many from the old days?"

She laughed. "The old days! What people d'you mean?"

"Don't know. The people who were around him when I was. It *seems* like old days."

"I suppose it must, with you being away. There were some people who were around back then. Paul Keane was there. And there were some writers. Gillian Woodcock and Davy McGravy came."

"I thought they were living in Newcastle." In fact, I knew they were.

"I think they are. They're definitely not living in Glasgow, anyway. But they came for the funeral."

"I saw them in Newcastle a while ago," I said.

★

It was almost eighteen months ago.

I'd got a phone call. "Hiya, Kev. Davy McGravy here . . ."

"Davy? From *Glasgow*?" I hadn't seen him since I'd left.

"Well, Newcastle now. Been here for a year or so."

"What're you doing there?"

"My wife comes from here. I was hacked off with Glasgow, so we moved down."

"Same as myself."

"Aye. Guess who else is here? Living here?" he asked, and for a second I thought it would be Mike. "Gill."

"Gillian Woodcock?"

"Aye," he said again. "It's an exodus of writers from Glasgow, big man."

I laughed. "What's Gill doing there? What's this with Newcastle?"

"She just did a reading here and liked it. So she moved. It was her gave me your number."

"How'd she get it?"

"From a theatre in London, she said." That made sense; I'd just had a play done at the ICA. "I'll tell you why I'm phoning," said Davy. "I've organised a reading here on Tuesday night. D'you fancy coming?"

"To Newcastle?"

"Aye. You'll no' get paid, but we'll get your expenses. It'll be a good laugh. You can stay with me."

I considered. "Wait a minute. Tuesday. You mean a week tomorrow?"

"Aye."

"I'd like to. I think I'm free. I've got a gig tomorrow, but I think that's all. Yeah, I'll come."

The next night I was on at a run-down cabaret in Soho.

It was called the Ostrich Club and had just got going. It was in the upstairs room of a crummy pub. The compère was a guy called Leonard. He was a friend of one of the actors in my play and had asked if I'd do a spot.

The show started around eleven-thirty. Leonard did a warm-up, then introduced me. The audience was rowdy but not hostile. I sang a couple of songs and read some poems. They laughed when they were supposed to and applauded when I'd finished.

There was a stand-up comic on after me. He was as funny as a black mass. I was sitting with a drink, feeling pretty pleased with myself, when Leonard came up to me. "You were great," he said. "Wicked. I don't know how long all the other acts'll last. You okay to go on again later if we need you?"

"Yeah. I don't mind."

I had planned to leave early; Peter and Francine were looking after David. But I felt like staying, and I knew they wouldn't mind. I felt relaxed for the first time after weeks of battles with actors and a director.

I went to the bar and got another drink. I was sitting down again when Leonard introduced the next act. "Let's hear it for – *Floozy Thompson!*"

I clapped along with the others as she got on stage. I'd heard her name or read about her, probably in *Time Out*. She was a tiny, hard-faced woman, not even five feet tall. Her bleached hair was cropped and she wore a nose-ring with a yin/yang symbol on it. Her face was pasty and her build stocky. She carried an acoustic guitar.

She didn't look at or speak to the audience. She just thrashed her guitar and belted out four of the most intense and captivating songs I've ever heard. They brought her back for an encore, which she did without acknowledging that they were even there.

Later, I was queueing at the bar when she got in line behind me. I smiled at her. "Your songs're great."

She grinned. Her face had a built-in sneer which made it impossible for her to smile. She could only grin. "I liked your poems."

"D'you do many gigs?" I asked.

"Not lately. Tonight was the first in months. Since my band broke up. I've missed performing."

When I arrived at Davy McGravy's flat in Newcastle the following week, Floozy was with me.

Davy didn't say anything when he opened the door. Neither did I. We just stood there laughing and shook hands. Then he stepped back and we followed him into the hall.

"So how're things?" I asked him.

"No' so bad. I'm gettin' some things published, at least." He laughed. "You're doin' okay."

I nodded. "Better than I'm used to."

We went into the living room. Marie, Davy's wife, sat in front of a gas fire. She got up and we hugged each other and she said I was a pig for not keeping in touch and I reckoned I probably was.

I introduced Floozy. "She's going to do some songs tonight."

"Great," said Davy. "Brilliant. It's gonnae be great tonight." He looked at me. "You singin' yourself, big man?"

"Yeah, I'll do a couple."

Floozy and I stashed our gear in a corner. I had a rucksack. She had two guitars and a canvas bag. When I'd asked about the extra guitar, she'd answered "Different tunings."

Davy fried up some fish fingers.

"Your diet hasn't changed," I told him.

"Fuck off. I'm the healthiest boy in Newcastle."

"Probably wouldn't be hard."

The three of them got steamed into the fish fingers while I had a slice of toast – white bread, of course. Davy used to be a Butlins camp cook.

Davy and I did most of the talking. "Gill's gonnae meet us at the pub," said Davy. "She'll be pleased to see you. I phoned Mike Illingworth and asked him to come, but he wasnae into it." He didn't seem sorry. He'd never been fond of Mike.

We got a taxi to the venue, a place called the Bar Point. It was the tackiest pub I'd seen for a long while, but there were plenty of people there. Davy went and set up the PA.

"We'll start about nine," he told us. It was about eight. He went up to the bar for a round of drinks, and I went to give him a hand. "So," he said to me, "what's the situation wi' you and the lassie? Which is to say, what're the sleeping arrangements?"

"Separate." Floozy had made that pretty plain. When I'd spoken to her at the cabaret, she'd agreed to come and play. When I phoned her to arrange it the next day, she'd forgotten – and sounded horrified when she answered the phone and I said it was me. When I asked if she still wanted to do the gig, she was so relieved that I wasn't calling to ask her out that she agreed without thinking about it. So, just to see how she'd react, I asked if she'd like to meet me for a drink that evening. She said she was too busy and I knew she was lying. Still, I didn't fancy her either. Much.

"So she *is* staying the night with us?" said Davy.

"Don't know. She's got friends in Durham. She says she'll make up her mind later."

We got the drinks and went and sat at a table. Floozy went to the toilet three times in half an hour. "It's nerves," she said. "I'm always like this."

"I know how you feel," I said, but I didn't. At least, I didn't remember. I lost any pre-gig nervousness a decade ago.

"I'll go and set up," said Floozy, and went over and sat by the microphone. I watched as she unpacked her guitars and tuned them.

Just before nine the barman came over and told Davy that Gillian Woodcock had just phoned. "She says she'll be here, but she's going to be late."

Davy looked around him. "I think everybody else is here. We might as well get started." He looked at me. "If you want to start wi' some music – "

I nodded. "I'll open up, then put Floozy on."

"Right." He got up and went over to Floozy. She looked tense. He said something and she nodded.

Davy stepped up to the mike. "Right, without further ado, we're kicking off now. My name's Davy McGravy – " A ripple of laughter at his name – "and if you think that's funny you'll love what I'll be reading later. But first, here's a man I used to do a lot of work with in Glasgow a long time ago. You may have read about him recently. He writes plays, he writes poems, he writes songs – Kevin Previn."

Polite applause as I got up. I didn't bother with the guitar. I went to the mike and wailed out an a cappella song I used to do at the readings in Glasgow. I saw Davy smile and nod at the memory, and the audience liked it too. I can't sing, but I know what I'm doing with my voice. There was solid applause at the end of the song.

"Thank you. Now for some real music," I said. "Put your paws together for Floozy Thompson." I got down as she got up. I could actually see her trembling.

I went to the toilet, which was next door. As I went past the pub door a chubby woman in denim dungarees and a baseball cap came in. She had a folder under her arm.

"Hi, Gill."

She smiled at me. "I knew you were here. I could hear you singing from halfway down the street. I'd know that voice anywhere."

"I know. Like a knife scraping across a plate."

We hugged.

From next door came the sound of Floozy starting up. Gill looked surprised. "Who's that?"

"Friend of mine," I said. "Go through and listen. I'm going for a piss."

I went to the bog. When I came back, Gill was sitting with Davy and Marie. The crowd was stamping and whooping along with Floozy. "That's some voice," said Davy.

It was. They didn't want her to leave even after five songs. They seemed to have forgotten there was supposed to be a reading as well. Finally they let her go and Davy introduced the next performer, who happened to be me. I got up and did it and nobody threw anything at me.

Then it was a couple of local writers, then Davy. He went over well; he'd obviously become a local favourite. When he finished he said there'd be a short interval and he was sure that, if they asked her nicely, Floozy'd be happy to play during it. That was news to Floozy, but they asked her nicely and she did.

"You sure there's nothing goin' on wi' you and her?" asked McGravy of the one-track mind.

"There isn't," I told him. Then I added, "But I'm starting to wish there was."

I'd been chatting to her during the less interesting readings. And liking her more by the second.

After another couple of songs, she looked at Davy and mouthed "*How long?*" He gestured that she do one more.

The second set began with some more local writers. They were dire. Save us from people who think being miserable means they're sensitive. Floozy and I went and sat in the lounge next door and talked for a while. Then we heard Davy introduce Gill, who was headlining. We went back through to listen.

Gill's set should have been the best of the night. But as she preened and posed, I heard someone mutter, "A fat, sweaty little woman reading fat, sweaty little poems." I couldn't disagree. But she seemed pleased with her performance, to the point of doing an uncalled-for encore, and I remembered the overweight, self-effacing girl of ten years ago, with her nervous manner and brilliant poems.

Davy went up to the bar to get the fee for the reading. It wasn't much, but there was some money left after he'd paid everybody's expenses. "No point in sharing it out," said Davy. "We'd be better just havin' a drink on it."

Floozy had been packing her guitars. Now she came over and said, "Have I got time to get the last train to Durham?"

"How come?" said Davy.

"Some people I know live there. I can stay with them."

Davy looked at his watch. "The station's a fair walk, but you might make it if you get a taxi. But you're welcome to stay with us. You've earned a drink."

Floozy looked uncertain. "I know, it's just . . ."

I said, "If you like, you can get a taxi to the station. If you've missed the train, get a taxi back here. Davy'll see to the fares."

Pause. Then she shook her head. "I'll stay." She told me much later that she'd decided to stay because I hadn't tried to force her.

The pub closed and we went to a club. It was dark and noisy and crowded and you could only hold a conversation with one person at a time, taking turns to shout in each other's ear. The other writers went their own ways, leaving Davy, Marie, Gill, Floozy and me.

I talked with Davy while Gill spoke with Floozy. Marie, pissed, sat staring at nothing. We were sitting round a wobbly wooden table.

Davy was pleased with the reading. I wasn't sure. "It takes me back!" he kept saying. It'd taken me too far back.

Davy checked the kitty. There wasn't much left. We'd all been drinking doubles. He stood up and looked at us. "Same again?"

"Can you get me some cigarettes as well?" said Floozy.

"Aye, no problem." He went to the bar.

Floozy nudged me. "Thanks for asking me to do this," she bawled in my ear.

"You did us the favour," I bawled back. "I hope you'll come and play at one of my gigs."

She grinned. "Yeah. I'd like to."

A hand dropped on to her shoulder. I looked up and saw that the body attached to it was large, male and aged about twenty. He bent down, leaned on the table and said something to Floozy.

She smiled, said something I didn't hear and shook her

head. Gill and Marie were looking at me and looking worried. The guy hadn't moved his arm from Floozy's shoulder and his face was slack and sneering. He spoke again and so did she.

Davy came back with a tray of drinks. He put a pint of lager and a packet of Silk Cut on the table in front of Floozy. She looked at him and smiled thanks, moving her shoulder to shake off the guy's arm.

The arm stayed where it was.

Davy looked at me. "What's the crack?"

I took off my glasses. "If I give you the nod, hit that fucker at the same time as I do."

He nodded.

The guy was still talking to Floozy. I couldn't hear what they were saying.

Gill looked at me and shook her head.

Marie gazed drunkenly at the table.

The guy turned and looked at me. "*Got the time?*" He made it sound like a challenge.

I showed him my watch. He turned back to Floozy. I took off my watch and ring and put them in my pocket. I saw Davy do the same.

Gill leaned over and said something to Floozy, who nodded and went on talking to the guy.

I downed the drink Davy'd bought me.

The guy turned to me again. "Got the time?"

I showed him my bare wrist. "A minute later than it was when you asked me a minute ago."

He looked at us, taking it in. Davy sat glowering at him.

"Right. Sorry for asking so many questions." He turned back to Floozy and said something. She shook her head. He walked away.

We all looked at each other.

"What's wrong?" Floozy shouted in my ear. I felt her warm breath on my skin, smelling her lager and cigarette smell, the kind of smell that usually turns my stomach.

"I thought he was getting heavy with you."

"Nah. He was harmless."

I put my glasses, watch and ring back on. "He didn't *look* harmless." I looked at Davy. "I need another drink. Enough money?"

"Aye. I'll have one too." Everybody else had a full glass.

"I thought that prick was going to fly at her," I told Davy as we walked to the bar.

He nodded. "I could see you were pissed off."

"It's not jealousy," I half-lied. "Floozy can do what she likes. But he wasn't taking no for an answer."

As we went back to our table, we saw the guy looking over at us. We looked back at him.

We finished our drinks and left. We were all drunk. Marie was actually staggering, and nobody else was far from it. We stood outside the club, waiting for taxis. I was talking to Gill when I felt a nudge. Floozy handed me one of her guitars.

"Hold this," she said. I took the guitar. Davy had the other one. Floozy walked over to the doorway of the club, where the guy who'd come on to her earlier stood beckoning.

She took out a piece of paper, wrote something on it, and handed it to him.

"He doesn't give up," I said.

"Floozy's being too nice," said Gill.

"I think she's enjoying the attention," said Davy.

Gill nodded. "I think so. A little bit."

Floozy came back. "Right," she said. "We going?"

Gill got a taxi first. Before she left, we hugged each other and said it wouldn't be another ten years till the next time, though I knew it probably would be.

Another taxi took us back to Davy's. As soon as we got into the flat, Marie had a fit of hysterics. First she started laughing. Then she got so upset about not being able to stop laughing that she started crying.

Davy looked baffled. "What do I do?" he asked me.

"Get her to bed. She's just drunk and not used to it."

"What about you two?" he said as he led Marie out of the living room.

"Just get us some bedding," I said. "And a sleeping bag."

He did. Then he showed me how to fold the settee down into a bed. Floozy sat slumped in an armchair, nearly asleep. I went to the bedroom with Davy to say goodnight to Marie. She'd stopped crying and was quietly lying on the bed.

"How's Marie?" Floozy asked me when I went back to the living room. She was still in the armchair, eyes closed.

"She's fine. Just drank too much." So had I, and at that moment it caught up with me. I rushed to the toilet and brought up twenty quid's worth of Southern Comfort.

"You okay?" Floozy asked when I'd come back. She'd come to life, folded down the bed and was starting to make it.

"Yeah." I helped her make the bed. Then I began rolling out the sleeping bag on the floor. "Since you're a guest, you get the bed this time. If we come back, we toss a coin for it."

She shook her head. "Don't bother about the sleeping bag." She went to the toilet.

I stripped to my underpants and got into bed. I wasn't sure whether Floozy just meant she trusted me enough to share the bed. As she came back from the bog and turned out the light and came to bed, I lay curled up with my back to her.

Go to sleep, Kev. She's not into you.

She put her hand on my leg.

I waited for what seemed like a long time as she ran her hand over me, then I turned to face her.

I put an arm round her and we kissed. She didn't seem to mind that I stank of vomit and for once I could tolerate the smell of tobacco. We kissed.

"I've been raped twice," she said.

I held her against me. I could feel the warmth of her through the T-shirt she'd kept on.

"I'm not going to hurt you," I said, wondering how I knew.

Moira told me to say hello to Davy and Gill when I saw them next. That was about all she could tell me.

"I don't think you'll find out much more," she said as we left the Atholl. "Nothing much happened in the last ten years."

"Something should have."

"He was his own worst enemy," she said.

I waited with her till she got a taxi. It was dark and the wind was pretty near gale force. "Where're you staying?" she asked me.

"Bed and breakfast."

"You can stay with me if you like."

"Nah, that's okay. I've paid in advance, so I might as

well get my money's worth." I didn't fancy a night with Moira; I knew we'd end up talking about Helene. I was grateful that she said goodbye and got into her taxi without talking any crap about keeping in touch.

I walked along Renfrew Street. The wind tried to blow off my hat, and the hand I held it on with ached with cold. I still had someone to interview that night. And the only one I felt like talking to was Floozy.

Moira wasn't wrong about how little people could tell me. After the second interview, I went for a walk around before going back to the bed and breakfast. I went back to the Low Road, back to Raeberry Street and then walked down Maryhill Road to St George's Cross. Then I walked up St George's Road till I came to Cedar Court – three crumbling blocks of flats.

It was so cold. The wind screamed around the three buildings. There was nobody about. I stood there for a long time, looking at the middle block. I wondered if they still lived there. Robert Frost – I think – said that home is the place where, when you turn up, they have to take you in. If that's the case, then I was homeless until my mid-twenties.

I walked back to the bed and breakfast.

Eight

I don't appreciate nature. I hate it. Nature is about rotting away and dying. When I see a handsome man in his forties, I don't think he probably looks better and has more character than when he was younger. I know he's dying. I know the lines and the grey hair are signs that his body is wearing out. Natural death means that before you die you piss and shit yourself and can't remember things.

from *The Book of Man* by Michael Illingworth

HE WAS AFRAID of death, but terrified of decay. He knew he couldn't cheat death, but he tried to cheat nature. He had his heroin to help him.

I helped him type the final draft of *Thus Spake Andy Schuster*. Or rather I typed for him whenever he was too far out of his face on junk to manage it himself. He hadn't been on the stuff all that long, but the amount that he loaded into himself was unbelievable. He'd jack up at least twice a day. Often he'd inject speed as well, to keep the heroin from sending him into a stupor.

He was quite principled about his hedonism; he felt that time not spent taking junk or getting laid was time wasted. He liked his sex as kinky as he could get it. Although bisexual, he preferred women. But if he couldn't get a woman as the evening was getting to a close, he'd go after the best-looking man.

About a month after I'd met him, he was round at my flat. We sat drinking tea and talking about the chances of his book being published. He wasn't pleased with it, but he said it was as good as he was capable of making it.

Suddenly he said, "Have you ever had a homosexual experience?"

I'd have felt awkward if it'd been anybody but him.

I laughed. He went on looking at me. "Mike, fuck off." I laughed again.

"Well, you're getting nowhere with Helene." He got up from the chair he was sitting on and advanced on me theatrically. "You should look elsewhere."

"Yeah. Well, go and find me a woman, you rampant bastard." I looked at my watch. "And she'll be here soon. You'd better behave."

"Behave, nothing. If you won't bend down, I'm going out to look for some bum."

"Go, then."

"I think you're suppressing it."

"Yeah. Well, I'll let you know when I finally manage to admit it to myself."

He left soon after.

He was right about Helene, I thought. She wasn't into me at all. I'd been seeing her a lot, but she wouldn't so much as hold hands with me. I'd told her I fancied her, and got the familiar refrain:

"I *like* you, Kevin . . . You must believe that . . . I really do *like* you . . . But I just don't want to spoil a good friendship . . ."

Translation: she liked me, but thought I was a geek.

I had to eat my heart out over two or three boyfriends. I suppose it was thanks to Mike that we got together. I don't know whether that means I should praise his memory or dance on his grave.

She turned up at my flat one night, dribbling over herself. I let her in and she vomited on an armchair in the living room. Annoyed at the mess and thinking she was drunk, I started to say something sarcastic. Then I realised she was shaking quite violently.

I put my arms around her. "What's wrong?" She smelled of vomit and of something else I couldn't quite identify. I could feel her shaking against me. "What's wrong, Helene? Are you ill?"

"I was round at Mike's," she mumbled, and I knew.

"You took some junk."

By way of reply, she was sick over us both.

I led her through to the bathroom and positioned her over the toilet. She puked some more, then spent a long time retching and bringing up nothing. I couldn't think of anything to say. I just stood behind her, holding her long blonde hair back from her face, out of the way of the puke and snot and saliva.

Finally she stopped retching and wasn't shaking so badly.

"Okay?" I asked her.

"Yeah," she rasped.

"Want to have a bath?"

"Yeah. Please."

I ran her a bath. I gave her one of my shirts and a pair of jeans. "I'll leave you to it," I told her. "Give me a shout if you need anything."

"I will. Thanks, Kevin."

While she had her bath, I took off my own puke-splattered clothes and had a wash at the kitchen sink. I'd just put on some clean clothes when Ivan, one of my flatmates, came in.

"Dear, dear." He sniffed the air. "Have you and the contents of your stomach fallen out again?"

"No. Helene's ill."

"Helene? Is that the girl you – "

"Yeah. She's having a bath. She was sick all over herself. And over me."

"So I smell." He made himself some coffee. "Right, I'm off to my scratch." He leered at me as he went out. "Best of luck."

I drank some tea and thought about Helene and thought about Mike and thought about throttling him.

Helene came in, wearing my shirt and jeans. Her hair was wet and tangled. "Have you got a hair-dryer?" she asked me.

"No. Sorry." I ran a hand over my quarter-inch crop. "Don't have much use for one."

She towelled her hair.

"Want some tea?" I asked.

"Mm. I'm not sure. I don't want to be sick again."

I poured her a cup. "Try some."

She did, and wasn't sick. "Can I lie down somewhere? Just for a while? I feel pretty wobbly."

We went to my room and she stretched out on the single bed.

I still had the smell of vomit in my nostrils. I lit a stick of incense, then went and sat on the edge of the bed. She lay on her side, facing me.

"Why'd you take the stuff?" I asked.

"Just wondered what it was like. I went round to see Mike, and he took a fix in front of me. I asked if I could have some. I just wondered what it was like."

"Did you shoot it?"

"Uh-huh. Not in the vein. Just in the skin. But it made me so sick I got scared."

"Didn't Mike tell you it'd make you sick?"

"He said it always makes you sick the first few times you take it. But he said you don't *mind* being sick. But I minded. I didn't feel anything else. I just kept being sick and I got really scared." She laughed. "I was sick on Mike."

"Copy-cat. I was there first."

"At least I didn't punch him." She looked at the candle in a bottle on the bedside table. "Can I light the candle?"

"Yeah, of course." I stood up. "I'll do it."

"No, I'll do it." She laughed. "I *like* lighting candles."

She sat up, lit the candle, then got up and turned off the light. She seemed shaky as she walked back to the bed.

"You okay?" I said.

"Yeah." She sat beside me and gave me a strange look. "Just a bit weak. But the bath did me good. I smell better now. See?" She held her fingers to my nose.

It took me a few seconds to realise, to recognise the smell, to know where her fingers had just been. Then she parted my lips and pushed her fingers into my mouth.

It was like an electric shock. My whole body seemed to spasm, then to tremble, to vibrate like a tuning fork. I sucked at her fingers until she pulled them away, and then we were sucking each other's tongues as we lay down on the bed and we were pulling off our clothes and then there was the hot shock of her bare tits against me and I clung to her and I thought I was going to faint.

Then we lay and held each other and kissed very gently

for a long time. I ran my hand over her tits, across her stomach and groin. She still had on a pair of knickers and they were wet.

I kissed her neck. "I want to kiss every inch of you," I whispered.

She smiled at me in the candlelight. "Go on, then." She turned over on to her stomach. "Go on, then."

I eased off her knickers, then took hold of one of her feet and kissed it all over, sucking her toes. I kissed her ankles, calves, knees, thighs, arse. Her breathing became heavier as I kissed my way from her spine to her shoulders, then licked and sucked at the side of her neck. She moaned and turned over on to her back. We kissed desperately, tongues licking teeth, teeth tugging at lips. I was shivering slightly as I went from North to South, kissing her throat, her tits – pausing to suck at each one – her belly, licking at her navel, finally arriving at her cunt.

She smelled slightly of salt, slightly of cinnamon, and entirely of herself.

With my tongue I searched for her clit and found it. She got very wet and started to moan.

Suddenly, abruptly, she pulled my head out of her depths and told me to lie beside her.

My face was dripping with her wetness. She kissed me, licking it off, gasping at the taste of herself.

"Look," she said. "Here's how I like it." She took hold of my index finger and began to lick it, very slowly at first, teasingly, then faster, harder, in circles.

"Got it," I said and went back down.

When I thought she was close to coming, I stopped licking, came up for air and lay next to her. She kissed me deeply, making little noises into my mouth.

I was still wearing my underpants. I took them off and threw them away. Helene kissed my chest and stomach.

"I want to fuck you," I said.

She pushed me on to my back. "*I'm* going to fuck *you*," she said, then bent her head and began to lick my cock.

I stroked and tugged at her tangled blonde hair as she licked the entire length of my cock, then drew it into her mouth. I thought I was going to come but I didn't. She knew what she was doing.

After a while she knelt between my legs and smiled at me. I realised she had a condom in her hand. I hadn't seen her get it. More quickly than I knew was possible, she covered my cock with the condom, then sat on it, straddling me, pulling me into her.

She gave a long moan and I knew I was going to come.

I grabbed her by the hips and held her still.

"Don't move," I said. "Don't move until you're ready to come."

She licked her fingers, then reached down and touched her clit. She moaned again and began to move on me, back and forth, moaning, filling herself with me. I lay underneath her, gasping, whispering her name again and again, repeating it like a mantra.

"I'm going to scream. I'm going to *scream*," she said, then she did, and I lost control and I came so hard my ears popped.

We held each other tightly, waiting for our breathing to slow down, in time with each other. The candle flame was steady, still.

*

Davy McGravy gave me an I-told-you-so smirk when he found me in bed with Floozy. It was nine in the morning. He came into the living room after knocking, and when he saw us he nearly dropped the two mugs of tea he was carrying.

"Straighten your face," I said, taking a mug from him. He handed the other to Floozy.

"Sleep okay?" he said innocently.

We'd barely slept at all. "Go and make us some breakfast, cretin," I told him.

He laughed. "Aye, okay. What d'you want?"

"Nothing for me," said Floozy. "I won't have time. I'll have to get back to London. I've got a gig tonight."

Davy nodded. "I'll phone you a taxi to get you to the station." He looked at me. "You heading off as well, big man?"

"No," I said, though I'd have liked to. But I didn't feel I could. "I'll get a train later. There'll be one in the afternoon."

Floozy left about half an hour later. Davy went out of the room to let her get dressed. I was still in bed.

"When'll I see you next?" I asked as she finished tying her shoes.

"Don't know." She came over and kissed me. "I'm doing a gig tomorrow night at the Ostrich. You could come along."

"I will."

"You could read some poems there."

"Yeah. I'll see."

She kissed me again. "See you."

After she'd gone, I got up. Davy made some porridge and

we sat in the living room and talked. Marie was still sleeping off the previous night's binge.

The longer we talked, the more I wished I'd left with Floozy. I'd known this would happen, but thought that to leave so suddenly after our first meeting in ten years would've been almost an insult.

Davy wasn't talking to me. He was talking to his memory of me. The past is always picturesque. He was still in love with everything – or nearly everything – I'd left Glasgow to get away from.

Finally I said, "Davy, if I needed all this I'd move back to Glasgow. Tell me what you're doing *now*."

He'd talked about the past for two hours. Now he filled me in on his present. It took five minutes.

There was a train at two. I left Davy's at noon, saying I wanted to walk around and clear my head. He didn't suggest coming along. I remembered how we used to sit up all night talking and then go for a walk and have breakfast somewhere. I felt sad.

Davy said he'd come and see me in London soon, but I knew he wouldn't. We shook hands and I said to tell Marie goodbye.

I was halfway down the street when I looked back. Davy was still standing at the door. He grinned and waved and shouted, "*Good luck with Floozy.*"

Newcastle's a grim place. The overcoat I was wearing attracted stares from passers-by. Nobody wears a coat in Newcastle, no matter how cold it is. This was a day in December, but still there were people walking around in T-shirts. If you wear a coat in Newcastle, you're a Soft Soothaan Bastaad.

I went into a café near the railway station and had some

tea. Outside it began to snow. I thought about Floozy and the lifestory she'd given me the night before.

The name wasn't her own creation, but it had stuck. I now know her original name, but she hasn't answered to it for years and so there's no point in mentioning it here.

She'd left Manchester for London when she was an eighteen-year-old punkette. She worked as a chef and fucked any guy she fancied. Then she fell in love and stayed faithful for a while.

Then she heard that, when she wasn't around, the guy often called her a floozy – even the punks had their double standards. She confronted him and asked if he'd been joking. He admitted that he hadn't.

That was on the day of her first ever gig, the open mike spot at a cabaret. She was so down she wanted to call the gig off, but it had taken so long to screw up the courage to do it, she was afraid she might never manage it again. So she went ahead. She was still seething with contempt and rage and hurt when the compère asked her name. "Floozy Thompson," she answered.

She was to regret it. The gig went well, she got other gigs, and Floozy Thompson it was. When she tried to revert back to her original name, people laughed. Such were the times.

Popular as she was, she encountered a lot of reverse snobbery on the punk scene because she could actually play her instrument. Her case wasn't helped by the fact that she could sing beautifully and her songs weren't negative. She got critical acclaim but no record deal. Eventually she got so pissed off she quit and moved to Cardiff and got a job as a chef in a hotel.

There was a guy there who worked as a waiter. She didn't really know him except to say hello to. One night he turned up at her flat with two friends. She invited them in, they all got pissed together and the guys raped her. Then the others left and the guy she worked with buggered her. As he left, he warned her that it was her word against theirs, and if she said anything to the police it not only wouldn't stick, they'd come round and do it again.

She didn't say anything to the police. What she did was start sleeping with the guy voluntarily. He probably couldn't believe his luck. When he wanted a convenient fuck, there she was. When he got tired of her and told her to piss off, she would always be there the next time he wanted her.

After a few months, she suddenly wondered if she'd lost her mind. She quit her job and went back to London. On her second day back, she went to a party. She was raped in a bedroom by a guy who'd played bass for her when she'd been gigging.

For the next year and a half, she slept with any man who'd have her, whether she fancied him or not. She reckoned she must have made a pass at any man she met in any context, regardless of age or appearance. Finally, knowing something was badly wrong but having no idea what to do about it, she swallowed her pride and went back to her parents' place in Manchester.

Her mother was glad to see her, but her father didn't want her living in the same house as him. Her mother was horrified to hear what'd happened to her. Her father said it was her own fault. He owned a flat in Salford, on the outskirts of Manchester. He rented it to Floozy at the same price he'd have charged anybody else.

One night, her father let himself into the flat without

giving her any warning. He found her in bed with a guy she'd been seeing for the past few weeks.

He evicted her, giving her a month's notice to quit.

She went back to London. She got a job and within months had written some songs. This time her songs were as bleak, as negative, as the punks could want. But punk was fading away as it became a marketable commodity.

Floozy began gigging again anyway.

I went along to Floozy's gig at the Ostrich Club the following night.

For no reason I could really understand, I felt nervous. When I'd slept with her at Davy's, I'd made some lame joke about the next time. Kissing me gently, she smirked and said, "How d'you know there'll be a next time? What if I just fancied it for tonight?"

Trying to sound unconcerned, I said, "Well, if that's all you want obviously I've got to accept it. But I hope it won't be just for tonight. I really like you."

If I could kid her I couldn't kid myself. I couldn't believe the feeling of dread I had at the thought of not seeing her again. *Grow up, you fuckhead.*

"Yeah," she said. "I like you too."

The club was crowded when I got there, even though it'd be a while before the show started. The place was dark. Candles in grimy bottles flickered on the grubby tables. Floozy was sitting with a bunch of people at a table in a corner near the stage. She saw me and smiled and waved.

I was heading towards her when Leonard waylaid me. "Hiya, Kev. You going on tonight?"

"I wasn't planning to, but I will if you like."

"Yeah. Yeah. Wicked." He had a stupid, kicked-dog look on his face and always seemed stoned when he wasn't. "You just come along to see Flooze?"

"Yeah." *News travels fast.* "If you want me to do a spot, make sure I'm on early."

"Yeah. Yeah. Wicked . . ."

I went and joined Floozy. She smiled and seemed pleased enough to see me, but she didn't seem about to turn somersaults. There were no seats free, so I sat on the floor in front of her chair. She introduced me to the crowd at her table, all of whom I forget except her flatmate-cum-roadie, Chas.

For the first time since I was about twelve, I felt shy. None of Floozy's friends spoke to me, and I couldn't bring myself to initiate a conversation. Floozy wasn't particularly attentive towards me, and I felt a huge relief when she finally put her arm on my shoulder and bent and kissed the top of my head. I looked up and smiled at her and leaned back against her thigh. At that point Leonard came on stage and introduced me.

I kept my set short. I did some poems from memory and made the audience laugh. In my bag I happened to have a copy of my only published play at the time. I plugged it, then read a short monologue from it.

"Thank you. You've been . . . an audience," I said and took a bow. When I left the stage there was no sign of Floozy. Chas said she'd gone to the dressing room to get ready.

I didn't stay at that table. The only one I could talk to was Chas, but his Irish boisterousness was turning ugly as he got drunker. He was a big guy, and I didn't like the thought of what might happen if he got annoyed at me.

I excused myself and went and stood at the bar and hoped somebody might arrive that I knew. Nobody did. Floozy came on and played. When she'd finished there were a lot of people wanting to talk to her, and it was about an hour before she came over to where I was standing.

"Can I borrow that?" she asked me, pointing to the book I'd read from, which was sticking out of my jacket pocket.

"You can have it." I signed it for her, *For Floozy, all the love in the world – Kevin Previn.*

She put it in her pocket without looking at the inscription. "Thanks. I'll read it tonight."

"I was hoping you'd come home with me tonight."

"I can't. Chas is really depressed. I'll have to talk to him."

"What's he depressed about?"

"A lot of things. He's in the Merchant Navy. He's got to go to sea again in a couple of weeks' time, and he doesn't want to."

"Oh."

"I'll see you tomorrow."

"Okay. When and where?"

She hesitated. "Don't know. I'll phone you in the morning and we'll arrange it."

"Okay." *You're not going to phone.*

Chas wandered over to us and gave me a drunken hug. "You were fuckin' brilliant, Kev. The best . . ."

Floozy looked at me with sudden coldness. "Go, will you?" she said quietly.

"Right. Call me if you want."

The night was made of concrete and frost. I zipped up my jacket and jogged to the tube station to warm myself up. *She's not interested. Just let it go.*

She rang at seven-thirty next morning.

"Hi. It's me."

"Who's me?" I mumbled.

"Floozy. Did I wake you?"

"Yeah."

"Sorry."

"S'okay."

"Do you want to meet up tonight?" she said.

"Yeah. Where?"

"It's up to you."

"D'you know the Scaramouche?"

"Yeah. I'll meet you there. What time?"

"About eight?"

"Yeah, fine." She paused. "I read your play."

"What d'you think?"

"It's brilliant. I wish I'd seen it. It's one of the best things I've ever read."

"Thanks."

"See you tonight." She hung up.

I was dozing off again when David came into my bedroom.

I grinned at him. "Morning, my man. What's up?"

He looked at me drowsily. "The phone rang."

"I know. I answered it."

He yawned.

"Still tired?"

He nodded.

I turned back the duvet. This was a ritual. "Come on," I said.

He got in the bed with me. His eyelashes were sticky with childish sleep. I rubbed it away with my fingers. He smiled at me. I smiled back. We both slept.

The Scaramouche was a tacky, surprisingly well-frequented pub, popular with social workers and old hippies. I didn't much like the place, but I'd picked it because it was quite near my flat in Tufnell Park.

As I went in the barmaid, Avril, called to me. "Hi, Kevin. There was a phone call for you about five minutes ago."

"What message?"

"No message. She didn't leave her name. Just asked if you were here."

Nobody knew where I was except Peter and Francine, who had David for the night, and Floozy. I rang her on the payphone and got her flatmate, Jo.

"Hi, is Floozy there?"

"No. She's over at the Oyster Bar. D'you want the number?"

"Yeah, please."

The Oyster Bar was where Chas worked in the kitchen. I phoned and when I asked for Floozy, it was Chas who came on. I gathered, from the fact that he was honking drunk, that he'd finished work for the day.

"S'at Kev?" he demanded.

"Yeah, Chas, it's me. Is Floozy there?"

"Naw, she's onner wayter meetchur." He sounded oddly sad. "Don' worry about anythingk."

"Okay. It's just that there was a message from her, or rather no message, and – "

"Don' worry, okay?"

"Okay, Chas. See you later."

"Just don' you worry . . ."

I said goodbye and hung up.

I sat at the bar and drank a Southern Comfort. I was busy listening in to the conversation around me when a pair of arms slipped around my waist. It was Floozy, wearing pink pedal-pushers, a tatty denim jacket and a drunken grin.

"Hi." I kissed her.

"Hi," she said. "I'm pretty drunk."

"So I see. D'you plan to get drunker?"

"Yeah."

"What d'you want?"

"Lager."

I got a lager and another Southern Comfort and we went and sat down at a table. "I hear you phoned this place," I said.

"Yeah." Pause. "I hope you don't mind me being pissed."

"Not at all. I like to avoid sobriety whenever possible."

"D'you drink because you have to?"

"No. I'm a volunteer."

"I got pissed because I was nervous about coming to meet you."

"How come?"

"That's why I phoned here. I wasn't going to come. I was going to call off. But Chas made me come. I was at the Oyster Bar with him, and he said if I didn't come and meet you he'd drag me to a taxi and come here with me."

"How come? Why were you going to call off?"

"Just nervous."

"Yeah, but why were you nervous?"

"Don't know. Well, I do know." Another pause. "I think it's because I really like you."

"Why're you nervous about that? I really like you."

She surprised me by grabbing me and kissing me long and hard, probing my mouth with her tongue. When she let me go she said, "I don't really know. I'm not nervous now. It's just that I didn't want to like anybody that much."

"I'm not a health hazard."

"I know. I trust you. But I was still nervous."

"Why?"

She grinned at me. "D'you like my baseball boots?" She lifted her feet and placed them on my lap. Her baseball boots barely existed. There were huge holes, through which you could see her bare toes. A long rip ran along the outer side of the left one.

"Lovely," I said.

"What the well-dressed bag lady is wearing this season." She thrust her toes through the holes and wiggled them. I took hold of her big toe and tweaked it.

And suddenly we were sitting there grinning all over our faces, not caring or even realising how ridiculous we must have looked in that crowded pub, just grinning at each other and contemplating Floozy's anaemic-looking toes.

"I *love* my baseball boots," she said, and we laughed together and she took her feet off my lap and put her arms around me and we hugged each other and we kept laughing and we were like kids and it was good.

The night got weirder. A woman collapsed on the floor,

clutching her heart. She must have passed out as she fell, because she took the weight of the fall on her forehead, then rolled over on to her back. Her friend knelt next to her and shouted for somebody to get an ambulance. Nobody moved. Everybody in the place just carried on drinking and talking.

"*Somebody get an ambulance! She's ill!*" her friend screamed. Nobody moved. Her friend stood up and ran out the door.

I got up and went over to where the woman lay. She was fortyish, with grey creeping into her brown hair. She seemed to be conscious.

"What's wrong?" I asked her. "Is there anything I can do?"

She sat up. "Go fuck yourself, you Scotch git," she told me. Then she lurched to her feet and, still clutching her heart, stumbled towards the door. I made to go after her but one of the barmaids beat me to it. She led the woman outside, whether to take her to hospital or dump her in the gutter I never found out.

I went back to Floozy. She was very drunk. "I don't like this place," she said.

"Neither do I. Want to leave?"

"Yeah."

"Drink up and let's go, then. It'll be closing soon anyway."

Outside it was black and freezing. I took Floozy's hand. She took my arm and put it round her shoulders, putting her own arm round my waist. We walked.

"We must look pathetic," she said, happily.

"Yeah." I bent and kissed her cold nose. Her head barely reached my chest.

"You live near here?"

"Yeah," I said.

"Is it okay if I crash at yours?"

I laughed. "I think I can stand it."

"We can't sleep together."

"Well, I plan to get all the sleep I need."

"Yeah, but – "

"You mean sleep together in the Biblical sense."

She laughed. "Yeah."

"How come?"

"I've got thrush. I just found out today."

"Oh, shit." I didn't know exactly what thrush was, but I knew what part of you it affected.

"You might not have it," she said.

"I think I do. When I had a shower yesterday, there was a funny mark on my cock. I thought maybe we'd just been too vigorous, but – "

"Mm. Have you been itchy?"

"Not noticeably."

"Does it hurt when you piss?"

"No."

"I don't think it's thrush, then. We probably *were* too vigorous the other night."

I scratched my crotch. "Funny, all of a sudden I'm really itchy – "

She laughed. "Psychosomatic thrush. Don't worry. If you have got it, I've got some cream you can use."

"What is thrush, anyway?"

"A yeast infection. You can get it from sex, or from taking antibiotics."

"Can you get it from baking bread?"

She laughed, which was more than that one deserved.

Later, when we were in bed Floozy held my cock and balls in her hand as I stroked her cunt. "I want you in me," she said.

I slipped a finger inside her. She spasmed and whispered, "I thought about you and wanked all day . . . I want you in me . . ."

As I slid into her sticky wetness she murmured in my ear, "Don't worry. Remember, I've got the cream."

I didn't catch it, though.

Nine

You fuck and you call it making love and maybe it is. But you pretend that you're together, that you're sharing the same thing. The truth is that you're no closer than someone watching a film in Odeon One, and someone next door in Odeon Two, watching a different film.

from *The Book of Man* by Michael Illingworth

HE WAS A GENIUS, but his life didn't amount to much in the end. So much for all the striving. Not that he ever strived too hard.

But now I know his rants about the ineffectualness of writing to be justified. He was more or less forgotten, even by the people he'd had the most influence on. Moira was typical. It wasn't that people had disliked him towards the end. Nobody had thought about him very much.

He'd written two books, one of them great. But now he was dead and he was just a guy who'd written two books and who nobody thought about very much. The books were still being bought and being read and then being put on the shelf and making no difference to anything.

At first, he thought he could make a difference. He certainly made a difference to me; within a few months of meeting him, I was back on the dole. I was also writing. Both were because of Mike.

I'd been writing, on and off, since I was about seven years old. The first thing I ever wrote was a story adapted from a James Bond film I'd just seen. I showed it to my parents and they said my handwriting was a mess and I'd better not be "writing daft wee stories" instead of doing my homework. I couldn't tell them that "daft wee stories" is the established literary form amongst seven-year-olds.

I stopped showing my stories to my parents but I didn't stop writing. I didn't write much, though. Unlike Mike (all comparisons go back to Mike), who began writing when he was twelve, never stopped writing and never wanted to be anything other than a writer, I hardly wrote at all. I didn't write often enough even to call it a hobby. But I did write. Once or twice a year, I'd start writing something, though I never finished anything.

Until I was about sixteen, the stories I'd start writing were simplistic adaptations of adventure films I'd seen. That was when I was still too ashamed of my miserable situation to face it, and I wrote for the same reason I went to the cinema.

When I was sixteen I stopped writing prose, partly because it seemed like too much work and partly because macho romanticism didn't make me feel better anymore.

Instead I wrote the odd poem, usually based – very obviously – on a bad pop song lyric. And I never realised how bad it was, because I never showed it to anybody.

I hadn't written anything for about two years before I went to Langside College. But the Higher English I was studying for somehow started me again.

And, somehow, my writing must have got better. Because

one night, when I was round at Mike's and we were drinking tea and he was reading out the just-completed last chapter of *Thus Spake Andy Schuster*, I finally said what I'd been wanting to say to him for months.

"Can I read you some stuff of mine?"

He looked at me, not getting it. "How d'you mean?"

"Some stuff of mine. Some stuff I've been writing. Some poems."

He looked surprised. "How come you didn't tell me you were a writer?"

I shrugged. "Don't know. I don't really write much."

He stood up. "I'll make some more tea first." Neither of us said anything while he made it. I got some poems out of my inside coat pocket. Mike poured me some tea and sat down again. "Right," he said. "Let's hear it."

I read him about ten poems. He didn't say anything until I read the second last, a poem about how I felt simultaneously grateful and angry towards him over what had happened between Helene and me – grateful that we'd got together, furious that he'd given her the junk.

"Not bad," he said when I'd read it. "You've got some good lines."

I read him another, the last one, a poem about Helene.

"I don't like that one as much," he said. "It's a bit waffly. But it's got some pretty good lines."

I've had more fulsome praise since then, but none that ever had the same effect. It wasn't important for him to enthuse about my writing the way I enthused about his, and he never did. He was always down on my writing, always critical, and that was because he thought I was a writer.

"*You didn't tell me you were a writer*," he'd said. Not, "You didn't tell me you wrote." However he felt about what I wrote, to him I was a writer, not somebody who wrote, not just a guy who'd been kicked out of school and had no qualifications and was just having a go at writing and trying the best I could. To him, I was a writer; that was the given.

And so I started writing every night. Usually I'd do a couple of hours when I got home from college. But sometimes, when my social life required otherwise, I'd come home from a party, drunk, at three in the morning, and write for an hour before going to bed. I never wrote anything worth shit at those times, but I still wrote. Because I was a writer.

At college, in class, I began to argue with the English teacher, telling him I didn't agree with him sometimes. I got into reading books more and more and respected his education, his English Lit degree, less and less. And, one day, I'd had it.

It was early in May, only a few weeks before the final exams. It was a warm day, really the first day of summer. I was sitting in the classroom listening to Lumsden, the teacher, go on about Louis MacNeice, who I had nothing against. But I was sitting near the window and that was probably what did it.

I was sitting there on a hard chair at a wooden desk and I was listening to phrases like Classical Structure and outside girls were wearing flimsy summer dresses and lonely guys who were still happy were going to the park to lie on the grass and read their books and this guy who was actually quite a nice guy was talking about Classical Structure and I just thought, "Is that it, Kevin?" and I got up and walked out.

Lumsden said something as I went, but I didn't stop to

answer him. What could I say? Not, "Sorry, I have to leave because it's a beautiful day and you're making a really good poet seem boring." He was too nice a guy to say that to.

I walked out of the class, nearly slammed the door, decided not to, gently closed it, and walked along the corridor. Then I realised I didn't know where I was going or what I was going to do.

I could go and sit in the refectory and have some tea, but suddenly I knew I couldn't be indoors. I went out the main door and down the old stone steps into the college grounds. It was about three o'clock.

The sun was taking his work seriously. I took off my jacket and walked to Victoria Park. A dog came up to sniff at me. I patted him, he decided I smelled all right, and went on his way. I put down my jacket and stretched out on the grass.

Looking at it from a particular perspective, you could say I'd really blown it. Since I'd got kicked out of school I'd had different jobs – been on a Youth Training Scheme (har-de-har-de-har), worked as a baker's van boy, labourer/gopher in a garage, in a factory putting lids on pies, as a gravedigger (that was dead good), as a bouncer at a disco, as a nude model for an art class (which I hoped would get me laid but didn't), as a shelf packer in a supermarket and – my main occupation – as one of the three million occupants of Maggie's paradise. You may be working out that I didn't have anything you might call a career.

I didn't think about it until I met this girl who was in her final year at university. I was so much in love I'd have used her shit for toothpaste. All the time we were seeing each other, she talked about university, and how she planned to go and work abroad when she finished her course. And when she finished her course she went to live abroad and for about six months I had a good penpal. Then I had an ex-girlfriend. I don't know which of us thought of it first, but somebody stopped writing to somebody, and then we both stopped writing to each other.

But she left me something. I read and re-read her letters and I couldn't settle. It wasn't her voice in the letters that did it – it was where the letters came from, the places she talked about – Marseilles, Florence, Toronto, Nebraska, California, Florida. I read the letters and in my head I saw movies with her in them.

And all the while I was still in Glasgow, signing on the dole and eating greasy food and walking around and waiting for something to happen. Eventually I knew that nothing was going to happen unless I made it, and in my present situation I wasn't capable of making anything happen.

So I went to a jobcentre, explained that I was unemployable, and asked about further education. They told me about Langside College. I went over there and spoke to one of the great and the good in a dingy office on a rainy afternoon. I was honest with him and he sympathised and I enrolled as a full-time student in the subjects I'd failed to qualify in at school – Higher English, History, Modern Studies, and O-Grade Biology and German.

I couldn't claim dole any more, so I applied for and got a bursary from the council – which arrived about three months after I'd started the course. Until then I survived partly on the goodwill of friends and partly by doing something I'm not proud of that belongs in another story.

I hadn't been a good pupil at school, and I wasn't a good student. I didn't like going to classes and I didn't like studying. But I went to classes and I studied. I knew I wouldn't get another chance, and so I sat through soporific classes and I took notes and I sat in the library reading grey and lifeless books and I took notes.

And, though not a good student, as the end of term approached I knew I'd learned enough to pass the exams. If I got good marks, I could go to university if I wanted. If I just passed, at least I'd be employable.

And I definitely would have passed. So now I lay on warm grass under a huge sky with the sun spreading itself across it and I knew I should go back to college and I knew I was never going to set foot in the place again. And I knew I was blowing it, all the work I'd done for nearly a year, and I was excited and I was worried.

But, mostly, I just felt good.

If I had to think about what to do now, it was good to think about it while I lay on the grass in a city park, stretched out and excited and loving the sun.

I couldn't really decide anything other than that I wasn't going back to college. As the afternoon turned into evening, it got a little chilly. I walked from Mount Florida to my flat in the West End, from one end of the city to the other. I wrote a letter to the college telling them I wasn't coming back; I didn't want to give myself time to chicken out.

I signed on the dole; they reduced my benefit because I'd voluntarily left college. I didn't starve but sometimes had to miss a meal. I certainly couldn't afford to go out at night, but I wouldn't have been going out much anyway. I was too busy writing.

I'd realised that if I was a writer then I'd better write. And I realised that if I'd walked out of college and left myself with nothing other than whatever possibilities being a writer offered, then I'd better learn to be pretty damn good at it.

So I wrote. I bought a second-hand manual typewriter and taught myself – with a little help from Helene, who'd learned at school – to touch type. And I wrote and wrote. I decided to replace student-time with writer-time. So during the day, when I'd have been at class, I sat in my room and wrote. In the evening, when I'd have been studying in the library, I wrote. I didn't even worry about whether the writing was any good – some of it was good, some of it was pretty duff and some of it sucked a big one. But that didn't matter. What mattered was that I wrote forty pages, sometimes more, every day. What mattered was that I wrote so much that sheer law of averages decreed that, by chance as much as talent, somewhere amongst it all would be something good.

It passed the summer nicely. I didn't see much of Helene during it all – she'd gone up to the Black Isle to visit some friends or do the Highland Fling or hunt the Loch Ness Monster or something – and though I thought of her a lot I didn't really miss her. I was happy and reassured by the postcards she kept sending me, but I was too far inside my own head to fret about not seeing her.

Most of the time I wrote in my room, but if I got bored I'd just go somewhere else. I still wasn't a brilliant typist and preferred to write by hand, so I could work anywhere: in the Mitchell Library, near-deserted with the students gone for the summer; in a café in Byres Road with sudden summer rain lashing down outside and people in T-shirts yelling and laughing and covering their heads with light jackets as they ran for shelter; sitting on a bench in the Art Gallery and Museum, with my notepad open on my lap, writing about and enjoying the cool dimness of the place after the hot, bright afternoon outside.

But mostly I sat in my second-floor room at St George's Cross. I sat at my desk with Helene's photo and postcards stuck to the wall above it and the heavy, smelly evening hanging outside the open window, and the sounds of the main road coming in. But sounds and smells didn't distract me and I just paid attention to what I was doing and I felt good.

Towards the end of July, something happened to drag me back into the real world. It was about one in the morning and I was on my way round to Mike's. I'd been writing all day and was pleased with what I'd done. I'd enthused about it to Mike when he'd interrupted me with a phone call. "I think I'm starting to get it together – "

"Why don't you bring it round and let me have a look at it?" he'd said.

"I'm not finished yet."

"Will you finish it tonight?"

"Yeah. I'm not going to bed till it's finished."

"Well, I'll be up till about four. Come round when you've finished it."

"Okay."

"If you're really late, just give one short ring. I don't want to disturb my flatmates more than I have to."

"Okay."

So at about one o'clock I was walking along Great Western Road, ring-binder tucked under my arm. The pubs had closed and there were quite a number of people on the street, heading home or standing around talking as they waited for taxis to take them to the clubs in the city centre.

At Kelvin Bridge I turned into Otago Street, where Mike

lived. As I did, I heard a shout from behind me. Two cops were walking towards me from Great Western Road.

"What's up?" I asked them.

"We saw that," one of them told me.

"Saw what?"

"Don't be fuckin' smart. We fuckin' saw it." They were advancing on me, backing me down Otago Street, away from the main road.

"Look, I'm not trying to be smart. I honestly don't know what you're talking about."

"Cunt. You pulled the mirror off a car."

"Sorry. I didn't."

"You did."

"Where?"

"What?"

"Whereabouts did I do it?"

He pointed in the direction from which they'd come. "Up there. In Hamilton Park Avenue."

"Sorry, but I came from the opposite direction. I live at St George's Cross. I just left there ten minutes ago. If you want to come back with me, my flatmate'll tell you."

"What're you doing along here?"

"I'm going up to see a friend of mine. He lives in this street." Suddenly, I hoped they wouldn't insist on coming up to Mike's to check my story. If he was stoned and they searched the place and found his junk, I didn't imagine they'd give him an easy time.

A long pause. The two pigs looked at each other. Then:

"Have you ever been in trouble?" I was asked.

"No."

"Well, you'd better get on your way before you do."

I turned and made to walk away from them, down Otago

Street. Turning my back was a mistake. One of them grabbed me from behind, pulling my jacket down over my arms, pinning them. The other one moved in front of me and punched me in the solar plexus with all his muscle-bound weight behind it.

The other guy let me go, and I dropped to the pavement, curled up, crying, trying to breathe through the pain.

I was yanked to my feet and shoved against a wall. I nearly fell down again.

"If you fall we'll kick you."

I clung to the wall, managed to stay on my feet. I tried to speak, but I was hurting too much and I couldn't.

"Want to spend a night in the cells?" one of them asked me.

I shook my head, not seeing them, clinging to the wall, looking at the ground.

"It'll cost you a tenner."

Only the pain told me I wasn't dreaming. I dug a ten-pound note out of my jeans and tried to hand it to one of them, but the effort cost too much and I dropped it.

"Prick," I heard one of them say, and something – a fist or a baton – smashed into my head. Strangely, it didn't hurt, but I lost hold of the wall and fell to the ground again.

A hand picked up the money – which lay on the ground near my head – but left me lying where I was.

"I said give one short ring – " Mike hissed when he opened the door. " – You've probably wakened the whole – Fuck's sake. What's the matter with you?"

"You're not going to believe this," I said as he helped me

into his room and laid me down on the bed. "I've just been mugged by two cops."

"Eh?"

"Uh-huh. Two cops just beat me up and took ten quid off me."

"Seriously?"

"As serious as my fucking gut-ache."

"Are you sure they were cops?"

"Yeah, I'm sure! They had uniforms, radios, the lot – "

"Are you sure the uniforms were genuine?"

"Yeah, I'm fucking sure! The uniforms were genuine, I could tell! *They were fucking cops!*" I was close to crying.

"All right." He sat down on the bed. "How hurt are you? D'you need to go to hospital?"

"I don't know."

"We'd better take you to casualty at the Western, then. Just to be sure."

I nodded and my head hurt. "Okay."

"Then we'll see what we can do about this."

I was so angry that I was actually crying. Mike walked beside me, saying nothing. It was about four in the morning and we were walking along Pitt Street and into Sauchiehall Street in the city centre.

We'd just been to Pitt Street Police Station. The sergeant at the desk had refused to even take my complaint. At first he'd just laughed at me, but when I'd persisted he'd turned belligerent and told me to leave.

"Look," I'd said. "I don't really care whether you believe me or not. I want it looked into. I'm not leaving here till you file my complaint."

He stood up. "Take a telling, son. Go home. If you don't fuck off out of here right now, you'll be staying here a lot longer than you were planning."

"On what charge?" said Mike.

"We'll think of something. And we'll boot the shite out of you while we're thinking."

Mike was for talking back, but I made him shut up and we left. I'd had enough experience of police methods of liaising with the community for one night.

As we walked up to the West End my head began to hurt again. My abdomen had never stopped. At the hospital they'd said I had a concussion and some bad bruising. When they'd asked what had happened and I'd said I'd been mugged, they'd wanted to call the police. When I'd given them the rest of the story, they'd decided not to bother.

"I can't believe this is happening," Mike said as we reached St George's Road.

"I'm telling you, it happened."

"No, not your being mugged. After seeing how that cunt back there behaved, I can believe they'd do anything. It's just fucking sickening that there's nothing we can do about it."

"There is. Write about it."

"What good'll that do?"

I said, "I'm going to write a poem about it and send it to the papers."

"Don't be an idiot. Nobody'll publish it."

He was right. Nobody would publish it.

The *Glasgow Herald* sent it back, saying they weren't

publishing any poetry at the moment. They made no reference to my covering letter explaining that it had actually happened.

The *Scotsman* rejected the poem without giving any reason. When I rang round the papers asking if they'd do something about it in their news pages, they all said I'd have to come up with some evidence. I knew the *Sun* would probably have run an article about it, but that would only have made sure nobody believed it.

I was sick with it. I couldn't settle to do anything. I couldn't muster any enthusiasm for writing. Helene was still away and I wished she was back.

What gave me the idea was Mike's book being turned down by a local publisher. He'd sent it to the Pictish Free Press, a small, arty company based in Edinburgh. It was promptly returned with a letter from Diarmid McDonald, the editor, saying he didn't like the book and thought it would work better as drama.

Mike was contemptuous, but I could see McDonald's point. Mike's prose was strong, and he wasn't interested in writing anything but prose. But his dialogue was fast and funny, and the story bordered on farce. When he read it to me, he read in different voices, gesticulating and pulling faces, giving life to the writing. And giving me an idea.

I spent a couple of days rewriting my poem about the police mugging, turning it into more of a dramatic monologue. Then I phoned Mike.

"I know how we can get a hearing for my poem. And for your book," I told him.

"Stand in the street and give copies away? That's what the Hare-Krishnas do."

"Well, there's nothing wrong with doing it that way. But it's not exactly what I was thinking of. I'm thinking of having a reading."

"By who? Just you and me?"

"You and me and some other writers, if we can find any worth listening to."

"How're you going to find them? Advertise in the personal ads?"

"If you're just going to take the piss, you can piss off and fuck your mother some more."

"Okay. Sorry," he said, laughing "How would we get people to come and hear it?"

"I haven't figured that out yet. But I will."

"What about a venue?"

"Leave it to me. I'm thinking about the Third Eye Centre."

"You won't get it. They won't give you the theatre for a reading by a bunch of unknowns."

"Leave that to me."

He was right. I couldn't get a venue.

The Third Eye Centre wasn't interested. Neither was anybody else. It was doubly frustrating considering that I'd found some young writers whose work I liked and who were enthusiastic about reading.

I'd scoured the local small literary magazines and phoned round writers' workshops. Glasgow writing for the most part was divided between couthy people with beards and tweed skirts lamenting being far away from the Highlands when a train would take them there in a couple of hours, and belligerent, bleary-eyed boys and girls who thought being a writer was all about drinking yourself into ill-health while taking easy knocks at politics in Glasgow dialect.

The former crew were impossible to contact, and I wasn't really interested in trying. The latter lot hung out in the Scotia Bar in Stockwell Street, where they gave readings and slapped each other's backs. It didn't take me long to realise I wanted nothing to do with them either.

But there were one or two writers who didn't seem to belong to either set. Davy McGravy was the pen name of a guy from Springburn who wrote plays and short, scathing monologues with a humour so grim that you laughed and then felt guilty for laughing. Gill Woodcock was an aspiring stand-up comedian who wrote comic poetry. She was almost pathologically shy and had never done a gig, but I gushed about how great her writing was until she agreed to perform.

The problem of getting a venue was solved when I phoned Tim McGuire, the Scottish Arts Council's associate literary director. McGuire was in his late forties and was one of Scotland's most famous living playwrights. He had been the editor of a counterculture newspaper in London during the sixties, and had been in the news for one reason or another ever since.

He was also an amiable and generous man, with an almost demented fixation with helping new writers. When I called him to ask his advice about a venue, he told me I didn't need one.

"It's summer," he said. "Have it in a park."

He offered to take part in the reading himself. When I went round to Mike's and babbled the news to him, he thought the idea was crazy. "You think people're going to come to sit on grass and listen to us reading? What if it rains? It's not Tim McGuire you need – it's Jesus Christ. Or maybe just a psychiatrist."

I wasn't deterred, and things happened fast. I decided to have the reading in a month's time, by the fountain in Kelvingrove Park. McGuire recommended a young poet named Stewart Greenwood, who lived outside Glasgow, in a small mining town. Greenwood didn't think it would work, but I told him about McGuire's involvement and he reluctantly said okay.

McGravy's wife, Marie, was a painter. She designed a poster, a line drawing of a figure sitting with a typewriter under a tree, and the words:

A LARK IN THE PARK –
WRITERS IN PERFORMANCE

and our names, McGuire's at the top, and the place and the date.

I didn't want to get any hassle from the dole – they'd probably consider this gig to be "work" and stop my money – so I put a jokey false surname on the poster. In future, as more and more people knew me as Kevin Previn, I would take it as my name. That wasn't the only reason, though.

McGravy, Gill and I went flyposting. Mike wasn't interested. He'd grudgingly agreed to turn up on the day, but warned that if there wasn't a fair-sized audience then he wouldn't read.

We covered the West End and city centre with posters. McGravy was on a Restart training scheme for the long-term unemployed and had access to a photocopier, so duplication had cost us nothing. He also photocopied handbills – just a reduced print of the poster – and, using the office mailing system, sent them out to two hundred people suggested by McGuire.

I didn't sleep much the night before the gig, though I was exhausted. I'd spent the whole evening until about midnight phoning people or going to visit them, just to check final details, make sure everybody knew they had to be there by noon, stuff like that.

It was one in the morning by the time I got to bed, and excitement and worry kept me from sleeping. I restlessly read for a while, then got up and went for a walk.

Since the incident with the two cops, I'd felt uneasy about being out by myself late at night, but I was determined not to give in to it. I walked along Great Western Road, down Byres Road and past the art galleries, then back to my flat. It was a warm night and you could smell the grass and trees of the West End and the sky was huge and cloudless and not too dark. I hoped the weather would stay like that.

It didn't. When I got out of bed at eight o'clock, after a few hours of irritable dozing, the blue sky outside was cluttered with dirty grey clouds. I ate a morose breakfast and prayed that they wouldn't leak.

Stewart Greenwood rang my doorbell at eleven. There was a sturdy coffee table in my room which I'd decided to use as a stage, and Greenwood, who had a car, had been roped in to transport it to the park.

There were about forty people – mostly friends of the writers – waiting by the fountain in Kelvingrove Park. Some journalists had turned up, and so had Diarmid McDonald from the Pictish Free Press and Teresa Ransgrove, director of the Scottish Poetry Institute.

People sat on the grass and drank soft drinks from cans

or tea and coffee from thermos flasks. It hadn't rained so far, but there was a brisk breeze, and I hoped everyone would stay till the end.

As it happened, the crowd grew. From the moment the first reader – McGuire, who also compèred – took the stage, more and more passers-by stopped, listened curiously for a minute or two, then sat down.

McGuire read some poems, even tap-danced a bit, then introduced me. During my first poem, I saw Teresa Ransgrove walk away, shaking her head, and I realised I wasn't about to become the darling of the Scottish Poetry Institute.

It got us a little publicity. Only one paper, the *Glasgow Clarion*, printed anything about it, but they gave us plenty of space. There was a photo of all the writers standing in a bunch by the fountain. The article praised Mike, McGravy and me, and quoted Teresa Ransgrove as saying we were "Just a bunch of creeps who use filthy language."

Diarmid McDonald contacted me and offered to publish a couple of my poems in the Pictish Free Press magazine. He also contacted Mike, giving him the names of some people he thought might be interested in *Thus Spake Andy Schuster*.

What happened, Mike? Why aren't we still doing readings together? Why aren't we regularly sitting up late over tea or home-brew, laughing at our young triumphs, and at how arrogant and full of shit we were?

Did you lie there in the dark amongst rows of other people nobody could help? And did you know when it was the end? Did you? Did you try to scream for help to the people who couldn't help you? And did the scream just whimper scared in your throat as you jerked your head and did you hear your hair scrape on the sterile white linen pillowcase?

Were you scared, Mike? Did you think about the people you loved and who loved you? Did you think about who loved you?

Did you piss and shit yourself and cry in the dark? Did it hurt really badly? Did you wonder whether I knew about it? Did it hurt?

Mike, I am so sorry.

Ten

Everything passes. However much pain you're in, you know it won't always be that way. However happy you are with the life you have, you know that sooner or later you're going to lose it.

from *The Book of Man* by Michael Illingworth

THE GRASS IN Kelvingrove Park was frozen a faded, anaemic green. There was no water in the fountain. It was too cold to sit on the park benches, let alone sit on the ground where the audience had sat for that reading long ago.

I spent about ten minutes there, walking up and down to keep warm, remembering. As with everything else on this trip, I wanted to feel awestruck and didn't. The park hadn't changed in more than ten years. The fountain, the trees, the shape of the big tree trunks, everything seemed just as it had been. And there didn't seem to be anything awesome about that, either.

The city had changed in other ways, though. Money had come to Glasgow, without diminishing the poverty of the majority of people who lived their lives there. I decided to go up to Maryhill, but it was too cold to walk there. So I took a taxi, which drove me past the city centre, where the money was.

The New Glasgow.

The wine bars with their Charles Rennie Mackintosh

designs and the blocks of expensive flats with locked gates at the entries to the private courtyards, the elegant shops and the lights installed by the river to make the city at night seem like "Paris on the Clyde" – it seemed like a sinister joke, like gaudy make-up on the face of a corpse.

The taxi took me to where the money wasn't. As we passed St George's Cross and started up Maryhill Road, I saw a man come out of a pub, drunk. I watched him as we waited at a crossing for the lights to change.

He had long black hair going slightly grey and a long goatee beard. He wore a padded anorak, ill-fitting jeans and training shoes. He walked with badly co-ordinated urgency, blinking in the icy afternoon light. For some reason he kept rubbing his forehead, pushing back his hair, but doing it so hard it was like he was slapping himself.

"Look at the state of that," I said to the taxi driver.

He laughed. "Aye. He's feelin' no pain."

"Fucking pitiful," I said. "You can just see it. Spend Sunday afternoon pissing it up in the pub, then go back to the house and your wife and your kids smashed out of your fucking face. Now they've got to put up with him till he sobers up or goes to sleep."

"Christ!" the taxi driver looked over his shoulder at me. "Who're you mad at, pal?"

I couldn't tell him. I couldn't explain to him why I wanted to get out of the taxi, grab the guy and slap his stupid drunken face and tell him not to go home and depress his wife and scare his kids, just to fucking go and sober up before he went near them.

I couldn't tell the taxi driver why I was angry. I wasn't just angry with some drongo staggering along the road drunk as a monkey's uncle – well, I was, but not just at him. I was angry with all of them, with the breweries, the bars, with everybody who won't say no to someone in that state. And I was so angry with the area of town that helped him be like that, I wanted to start hitting walls when I'd finished hitting him.

I got out of the taxi near the shopping centre with the adjoining dole office. I just walked around. I walked by the canal, so covered in green weed that it looked like you could walk on it. There were some teenage boys fishing for the tiny pike that somehow manage to live in the filthy water.

We used to fish there when I was a kid, too.

In that place, cruelty is encouraged. My best pal when I was ten was Peter O'Connor, a genial kid with awesome buck teeth who – in spite of his mother and father – somehow managed to be a nice guy. I hope he still is.

We always hung around together. Often we played with other kids, but always the two of us. We were a unit. You played with Kevin and Peter, not Kevin and maybe Peter.

One of the other kids we sometimes played with was Robert Baker. He was the same age as us, but older and younger at the same time. In Maryhill, the middens – brick sheds in the back courts where the bins were – were known as "midjies". And Robert was known as "Robert Baker the Midjie-Raker".

His midjie-raking was legendary. It was said that his parents didn't feed him. But he'd got so into raking through bins that feeding him wouldn't stop him. One winter evening a woman who lived up our close went to the midjie to dump her rubbish and caught Robert raking the bins.

"What the hell're you playin' at, son?" she demanded.

He didn't answer, just stood there among the bins, never taking his eyes off her as he ate the half-slice of stale bread he'd found.

"You don't need to do that. I'll feed you." She waited. He didn't answer. "I'll feed you. I've got plenty in the house. Come on to the house."

He went with her without saying a word. In her living room, as she fed him soup, sausage, egg and chips, all he said was "Thank you".

She gave him a bar of chocolate as he left, telling him, "Don't rake the midden again. If you're hungry, just come to me."

He muttered another "Thank you", as he ran off down the stairs.

Later that night, she looked out of her window into the back court. Robert was busy midjie-raking, shoving through the bins like a scavenging dog.

He played with us sometimes. Peter and I would go fishing in the canal, and sometimes Robert would come too. We never asked him about his midjie-raking and he never mentioned it. In fact, he hardly talked at all.

We didn't go fishing in the canal very often, because it was seldom that anybody caught anything there. The first dozen times we caught nothing. Robert would sit at the edge of the concrete basin, legs dangling over the side, cheap rod resting on his lap. He had thick black hair and a white spotty face and he always wore a black anorak and grey trousers.

Then Peter caught a fish. He was so shocked when he felt

the tug on his line that he almost forgot what to do. Then he began frantically reeling it in, shouting, "I've got a bite! I've got a bite!"

"It's just weeds," I said. Robert didn't say anything.

"It's no' weeds! It's a bite! It's a fish!" he yelled, saliva dribbling in excitement from his protruding teeth.

Then I saw that he was right. A small pike surfaced, feebly thrashing its dull, sick-looking body. All the fish in that canal looked sick.

I went as wild as Peter. "It is! It is!" I began to dance about beside him. "Lift it out!"

He lifted it out of the water just by raising his rod. It hung limp on the line, only its twitching gills giving any indication that it was alive.

"What do we do with it?" said Peter.

"You can't eat it," I said. "So you're supposed to take it off the hook and put it back in the water."

"I'm scared to touch it," said Peter.

"Well, I'm no' touching it," I said.

"Scared?"

"Aye. It might be poisonous. Anyway, it's your fish. You caught it."

Robert stood up. "I'll do it."

Peter manoeuvred his rod until the fish dangled in front of Robert, who took hold of it and took the hook from its mouth.

"Let's see your penny," he told Peter.

"What for? Don't kill it. Put it back."

"I'm putting it back. But let's see your penny first."

Peter took out his penknife and handed it to him.

"Aw, don't!" I said as I saw what he was going to do.

"Aw, fuck – " Peter said, aghast.

Robert ignored us. We watched as he cut both of the fish's eyes out, then threw it back in the water.

Nobody spoke as the three of us walked home. It was a summer night, just late enough to be turning chilly.

As we reached the corner of Mount Street, where we'd go our separate ways, Peter said, "You shouldn't have done that. It was my fish."

"You didn't want it. You were scared to touch it."

"But that was a rotten thing to do."

"Don't be a jessie," Robert told him.

"I'm away home," said Peter.

"So'm I," I said, and walked off along Raeberry Street.

I didn't see Robert for quite a while after that. Well, I saw him around quite often, but I didn't play with him. Then, towards the end of the summer, Peter and I hooked up with him again and he gave us a demonstration of his latest hobby.

The middens were infested with rats. They'd appeared in force during the months when the Cleansing Department went on strike and rubbish filled the back courts in stinking piles. When the strike was over and the rubbish was gone, the rats were still with us. They got so big that the tabloids began printing stories about "super-rats". For once they weren't exaggerating. They were true, the stories about huge hungry rats attacking babies in their cots, and fighting back like angry cats when hysterical mothers tried to drive them away. Nobody wanted to believe the Victorian horror stories under the banner headlines. But, in 1970s Glasgow, they were true.

Some might say that Robert just evened things up a little, scored a few points for the two-leggers. Others would say the rats were in as bad a situation as we were and so you couldn't really blame them.

Robert had a hamster-cage. It had housed a hamster at one time, and I don't even want to speculate about what happened to it. But with the hamster gone, the cage wasn't redundant.

He'd put a bit of rancid meat in the cage and leave it by the midden, with its door left open. He'd stand a distance away, but still close enough to see, and wait. It wouldn't be long until there was a rat in the cage, groping and gnawing at the bait. Robert would rush over and kick the cage door shut.

He didn't catch the biggest ones, the super-rats, because they couldn't get through the small door. But the ones he caught had plenty to offer him by way of amusement.

In the afternoons, he had the smelly two-room flat he lived in with his parents to himself. His father worked for the Cleansing (I swear it) and his mother had a part-time job in the local off-licence.

Robert would take the cage with the rat up to the flat. If the rat was lucky, it might get to finish eating the bait before Robert had boiled a pot of water big enough to fill the sink.

He'd pour the boiling water into the sink until it was nearly overflowing. Then he'd plunge the cage into the water and boil the rat alive.

Peter and I stood one afternoon in Robert's grimy kitchen and watched a rat swell to nearly twice its size, saw its eyes strain to explode from its head, saw a red-brown substance – maybe its tongue – come out of its mouth as it rolled around under the steaming water.

You could smell it on the steam. Even after we'd left the flat and were walking along the road in the sunlight, I only had to take a deep breath and I'd smell it again. The smell of boiled rat.

Maybe it wasn't that place that was the cause. Maybe it was Robert. Maybe he was just crazy. After all, Peter and I lived there and didn't spend our time raking bins or torturing animals. Robert was crazy all right. But does it happen in areas with detached houses and second cars and neighbourhood watch systems?

These queasy recollections didn't prevent me from getting hungry. Near Gairbraid Avenue I found a pub that served food and that looked like a stranger could go in and not get killed.

It turned out to be even better than that. I went in and found that there was a restaurant area separate from the bar. An up-market pub in Maryhill? Time marches on. I sat down at a table and a waitress-barmaid came over and I ordered macaroni cheese and chips.

The place was quiet, this being the middle of the afternoon. I guessed that the lunchtime clientele would be mostly staff from the nearby DHSS office. I drank some tea as I waited for my food.

Each time I'd seen Robert Baker demonstrate his alternative theory of pet care – first the fish and then the rat – I'd said nothing, just kept quiet and got away from him as quickly as I could. Because I couldn't cast the first stone.

About a year earlier, Peter and I were playing in the park called the Low Road. Peter had to go home early because his parents were taking him out somewhere. It was still early in the day and I didn't want to go home.

So, after Peter had gone, I carried on playing. I'd found a stick – about the length and width of a broom handle –

and for no reason I know of I kept plunging it into the River Kelvin. Maybe I was playing at spearing fish, like I'd seen Tarzan doing on TV.

While I was doing this I saw something floating underwater, something that looked alive. Except for minnows, it was the first living thing I'd ever seen in that murky, polluted water.

It was greenish-grey in colour, about the size of a man's fist. It was floating along just under the water's surface.

With one stroke I fished it out with my stick. It slithered off the stick and on to the grass. I looked at it. It didn't move. I wondered what it was; I thought it might be a frog, but it didn't look like any frog I'd ever seen on TV. I couldn't see any eyes or mouth and it didn't seem to have anything you could clearly define as legs. It was just a wet, slimy blob.

But it was definitely alive, whatever it was. I could see parts of its skin pulsating. It was definitely alive.

I swung the stick like a golf club, hitting the creature and sending it flying. It landed on the grass a few feet away. There were now spots of blood on its skin. I couldn't see any pulse.

I began to cry. I prodded the creature with my stick. It twitched once. Full of remorse, I wanted to carry it home with me and take care of it. But I couldn't bring myself to touch it. Instead, I used the stick to push it back into the river. It was swept away. There was nothing else to do in the park and I cried most of the way home.

I could never cast the first stone. Sometimes, when I stay up too late at night, the memory comes back along with other memories. And I stop what I'm doing and go through to the bedroom and get into bed with the woman I share my life with. And I cling close to her and I pray to everything there is and I ask it to take care of us because I'm only little and so is she.

Eleven

It's like staring at the summer sun; the longer, the harder you look at it, the blinder you become.

from *The Book of Man* by Michael Illingworth

I DON'T BELIEVE I'll ever understand what happened between Helene and me. I know she never did.

She was never able to tell me exactly why or when she changed her mind about me, and I asked her often enough.

"Don't know," she said one time. "It came in stages. I didn't even *like* you all that much when I met you."

"So how come you went out with me?"

"Morbid curiosity. Then I realised I liked you. Then suddenly I wanted you."

"What brought that on?"

"Haven't a clue."

"I don't know what you see in me."

"Yeah. It beats me, too." Then, seeing my mock expression of hurt she said, "But I fancy the pants off you now."

When she came back from her summer in the Highlands she couldn't believe what she came back to. Although I'd let on to her that I wrote poetry, I'd always been too shy to let her see any. Now I was putting it out for anybody who wanted it; some of it was published in the *Pictish Free Press Review*, and I was performing it all over the place. Although

Mike couldn't organise a wank at an orgy, Davy McGravy was as into it as I was and we were organising events in any pub or community centre that would have us.

Helene was bemused. I'd written to her on the Black Isle only once, and I hadn't told her much about what was going on outside my head. Now she was back, even more tanned than she had been, and she actually seemed glad to see me. In spite of all the postcards she'd sent, I'd wondered on and off if she'd feel the same about me after a three-month break.

It seemed she did. I met her off the train on a wet, warm afternoon and we went straight to my flat and fucked ourselves thin. When she went home to her parents' place that night, she forgot to take her rucksack with her.

And she never did take it away. Over the next couple of weeks she started moving things in. Each time she stayed the night with me she'd bring a bag or two and leave it. It was never really discussed between us, but gradually she moved in.

The time spent up North had made her realise just how little she missed her parents, and how much she liked being away from them. They hadn't been getting on for quite a while, but when you live in that kind of situation for long enough you get used to it. Now, having had a break from it, she realised she couldn't take it.

"I'm going to have to get out of there," she told me. "It never stops. When I'm in the house it's constant. 'What're you going to do with yourself? You have to do something.' I tell them okay, tell me what it is I'm supposed to do and I'll do it. So they say, 'It's your responsibility. You have to decide.' So what they're telling me is they don't want me to be the way I am, but they don't know the way they want me to be. As if I *like* not doing anything! And when I've been with you for the night, they start on about how I've been wasting time with you when I should be doing something – " she broke off. "God, I sound like a teenager."

"So move out of there."

"No money."

"You'd get Housing Benefit."

"Yeah, but to get a flat you need to pay a deposit, and a month's rent in advance. I don't have that. I saved some money, but that went during the summer. All I've got's what I get from the dole every fortnight."

"Well, you know what to do. Move in here."

She looked at me. "Are you sure?"

"How d'you mean?"

"Are you sure it'd be okay? You wouldn't mind?"

I laughed. "Come on. You practically live here anyway. All you have to do is bring the rest of your stuff and stop going round to your parents'." Pause. "Besides, I like having you here."

She grinned. "I hoped you'd say that."

There wasn't much of her gear that she hadn't moved in already. She brought her record player and black-and-white portable TV and some other stuff. Her father brought it round in his car. He didn't get out of the car, let alone help her carry the gear up to the flat.

I tried to help but she wouldn't even let me go down the stairs. "I don't want you meeting him," she said. I could see she'd been crying not long ago.

"Don't be stupid. If he wants to be a surly bastard, it's up to him. He doesn't have to talk to me; I could give a shit. But I'm not going to sit up here and let you do all the donkey-work on your own."

"I can carry it on my own. I'm not fucking feeble. If you go down there, he'll probably say something to you."

"Boo-hoo."

"I know what your temper's like. You'd probably thump him. It's not worth the bother. I don't care about him, but I don't want you in trouble."

So I stayed in my room and looked out of the window and watched her unload her stuff from the small red hatchback. Instead of carrying it upstairs item by item, she piled it all on the pavement by the front door. When she'd taken everything her father drove off, leaving her standing by her meagre hoard.

I went downstairs and started carrying things up to the flat while she stood guard over what was left. Twenty minutes later my room – always pretty cluttered – was like a storeroom.

I hadn't told my flatmates she was moving in. That way they wouldn't be able to object, and since Helene spent most of her time there anyway, I was sure they wouldn't mind once they realised it didn't alter the way of things in the flat.

I was right; it was a fortnight before any of them even knew she'd moved in, and that was only because he noticed her name had been added to the list of names on the door. They were all a bit peeved that I hadn't bothered to tell them – and they weren't wrong – but they were generally okay about it. The landlord wasn't happy about it, but the happiness of landlords never was my main concern.

Fucking her wasn't the best of it. For the first time in my life. Fucking her wasn't the best of it. The best of it was waking up in the morning to find her next to me, scowling in her sleep in the grey early daylight.

I believe she thought that she'd be happy. I believe she thought that if she got away from her parents and moved in with me her problems would be solved.

But one set of problems just gave way to another. Things weren't better for her. Nor were they worse. Just different.

Her parents had been on at her for having no focus, and she was still adrift. She watched as things happened for me and the only variety in the slow treadmill of her own life came when the dole hassled her to go on a training scheme. She never told me how that felt, but I believe I know anyway.

A woman at the dole told her that at her age she should be trying to conquer the world. But what if you haven't seen a world you want to conquer?

Finally they forced her on to a Restart scheme, the same one Davy McGravy had been on. It was in an office in the city centre and was supposed to teach you word processing skills while giving you valuable work experience, which is to say you went and worked for nothing.

But it had been bearable for McGravy. While hating the office, he'd exploited it. He'd used the computers to type his own work, used the Xerox machine to copy it, used the phone to call magazine editors and sent them his work through the office mailing system. On top of that, he pilfered all the stationery he could get his hands on, kitting out himself and all the other writers he knew with paper, notebooks, pens, staplers, and ring-binders.

For Helene, though, it wasn't a means to an end, or an inconvenient stopping-place on the road to where she wanted to be. There wasn't really anywhere she wanted to be.

Looking at it now, I know I should have been able to see how miserable she was. But at the time, whenever her frustration manifested itself, it always took me by surprise.

One Saturday evening about two months after she'd moved in, we were out for a walk and she was looking in shop windows and saw a print – an ink-drawing of the Glasgow art gallery and museum – that she liked. The print didn't cost much, but the shop was closed. I said I'd go there first thing on Monday and pick up the print for her.

On the Sunday I began to feel ill. By Monday morning I was so sick I could hardly get out of bed. Helene was at work in the Restart office and there was nobody else in the flat.

I wasn't registered with any doctor. In mounting panic, coughing so hard it hurt, I went through the phone book, found the nearest surgery, called them and asked for an emergency house call.

The doctor came round later that morning. I had an infected trachea. There was nothing I could do about it except rest and hope it went away without developing into bronchitis.

I stayed in bed for the rest of the day. The painful cough didn't seem so bad now that I knew I wasn't about to die. I passed the time reading, now and then getting up to go to the toilet or make tea and toast.

Helene got home around five-thirty. She had that swagger, and set half-smile, that arrogant people have when they're depressed.

"Hi," I said.

She dropped her bag, threw off her coat. She gave me a

look, said nothing, then sat down and began to take off her shoes.

"Did you get the print?" she asked me.

"No," I said. "I've been – "

I didn't get any further. She wrenched off a shoe and threw it at me. It hit me in the face, just under my left eye, and I saw fireworks for a second. I put my hand to the spot and it came away bloody.

"*You fucking bitch! What do you fucking think –* " She walked out, grabbing a pair of trainers as she went. I got out of bed to follow her but my head spun and I had to sit down. Then I heard the front door being closed, surprisingly gently.

My head cleared. I stood up and, satisfied that I wasn't going to fall over, went and looked in the mirror. The cut was tiny, but I knew it wouldn't be long before the eye swelled shut.

I boiled a kettle, held a hot compress to my eye for as long as I could be bothered, then went back to bed. Beyond my anger I had no idea how I felt. It was after midnight when she came back. I heard the front door open, then two voices coming from the kitchen, Helene and our flatmate Ivan.

As I heard her approaching our bedroom I put down the book I was reading and closed my eyes, pretending to be asleep.

She sat on the edge of the bed and touched my arm. "Kevin?"

I opened my eyes – or the one eye I was able to open – and looked at her.

"I'm really sorry," she said.

I didn't know what to say. I just nodded.

"God, your eye. I can't believe I did that."

"I was going to get you the print. But I couldn't. I'm ill. What d'you think I was doing in bed when you came in?"

"What's wrong with you?"

"An infected trachea."

"How d'you know that's what it is?"

"I had to get a doctor to come round. He says that's what I've got. He told me to rest. That's why I couldn't go out."

"I'm really sorry."

"Even if I'd just forgotten to get it for you, you still had no right to do that." I touched my eye.

"I know. I can't believe I did that. I'm really sorry."

I didn't know what to say. She went to the kitchen and came back with a pot of tea. She sat on the bed and poured me a mugful.

I said, "If that shoe'd hit me just a tiny bit any other way, it could've blinded me."

She nodded. "What it did do's bad enough. I'm really sorry." She started to cry, not hard, just sniffing and wiping her eyes. She was so beautiful and so full of everything and I felt so useless.

She came to bed and we lay and cuddled for a while. Finally she said, "I love being close to you." But she said it sadly, almost fearfully. And that's how such things are usually said, endearments made in a desperate voice. It's as if we're pleading with Fate or whatever not to take this fragile thing away, to let us have just this and let it be all right. Sometimes I'd hold her to me, hard, loving her, feeling her warm and solid, feeling so close to her, so *with* her, all the while knowing that it couldn't be for ever, that even if we were lucky sickness and death would eventually take us to a place where we wouldn't know each other again.

Diarmid McDonald had told Mike to send *Thus Spake Andy Schuster* to an acquaintance of his who was editorial director of a small publishing house in London. A couple of weeks after he'd sent it, he came round to my flat brandishing a letter. They'd accepted the book.

It was the first time I'd ever seen him out of bed at ten in the morning. I congratulated him and suggested we go out and have breakfast. Helene was at work, and there was a strange bleakness about the flat that Mike's news couldn't lift.

We decided to go to the Underground Gallery Café off Byres Road, a fifteen-minute walk. There was a thin drizzle and the streets and parks were thick with fallen leaves. I was tired and didn't feel up to talking much. That was all right; Mike talked.

"It's happening," he told me as we walked. "It's all happening. These people really seem to rate me. They – you saw the letter – it seems they're really into me – "

"Have you written back to them?"

"No, I phoned them as soon as I got the letter. They said they'd put a contract in the post today, so I should get it tomorrow. I want to get everything signed before they can come to their senses and change their minds."

"How much are you getting?"

"A grand up front."

"Not bad."

"Well, it seems it *is* pretty bad, but they can't afford any more. They're a pretty small outfit. But a grand'll be handy. Pay the rent and buy the junk for a few months."

"What's your next book going to be?"

"The guy at the publishers asked me that. I said I was working on another one, but I'm not."

"Are you going to?"

"Yeah, I suppose so. I haven't really been thinking about that."

"What *have* you been thinking about?"

"How this'll get my folks off my back and how I might be famous and all the people I'll be able to fuck."

I laughed.

"Which reminds me," he went on. "In the light of my newfound literary magnitude, I don't suppose you're prepared to touch your toes?"

"Fuck off."

"I'm telling you, everybody should try taking it up the arse just once. It's an exhilarating experience. You should try it. It'd do you good." He waited, got no spoken response, smirked and said, "Oh, suit yourself. Some day soon you'll realise what you've missed. Fanny and bum'll be falling over each other to get at me."

"I'll realise it too late, I know. But I'll try to live with the jealousy."

We arrived at the café. It was the kind of place Mike liked, a basement full of West End egos who drink coffee even though they hate it.

We had tea. Mike got even more manic, and filling him with croissants and doughnuts didn't calm him down any. We used the payphone to call Davy McGravy and Gill Woodcock, and they came over. As the afternoon wore on, tea turned into beer. In the evening Helene joined us in one of the half-dozen pubs we went through that day. By closing time all of us were drunk – even Mike, which was a rarity. He put us all in taxis to get home, and insisted on paying.

He phoned the following morning. I was still asleep, but Helene answered it. She was so hung over that she'd taken the day off work.

She woke me. "It's Mike on the blower. Are you fit enough to come and talk to him?"

"Did he say what's up?"

"Yeah. He's having a party tonight. He's booked the Western. Wants to know if we're going."

"D'you want to?"

"Yeah. Fine by me."

"Okay. Tell him we'll be there." I closed my eyes again. Helene laughed and went out.

At the party – in the back room of a pub near Mike's bedsit – I knew things were moving for both Mike and myself. The party was wild; I'd brought along my guitar and I sang some songs, famous ones and a couple I'd written myself. Mike told me he was starting another book and needed my help.

There was a guy at the party who ran a profit-share theatre company and had asked Mike to write a play for him. Mike said he wasn't interested in writing drama, but told the guy he should speak to me. He did, and we arranged to meet up the following week.

It got weirder and fuzzier. When Helene and I ended up fucking in a cubicle in the men's toilet, it began to seem like a good idea to call it a night and go home.

Twelve

The gods are cruel. Fate is cruel. Karma is cruel.
Whatever you believe in, you should know it's cruel;
and if you believe in nothing, then there's only
cruelty.

from *The Book of Man* by Michael Illingworth

I THINK MIKE panicked. He felt he had to do another book now, and he wasn't sure what to do about it. In his panic, he started writing *The Book of Man*.

Every day, he'd come round to my flat and read me what he'd written the night before. It was never very much; he was never prolific, and always lazy. He only wrote at night, and most nights he was too busy being debauched to write much. But, of the little he did write, a lot of it was good.

Mine wasn't. For some reason I'd lost it. Maybe it was because I was so preoccupied with what Mike was doing, I don't know. But I couldn't get it together myself. It's true that writer's block is a disease of amateurs, and I was too disciplined to be blocked. I wrote as much as I always did. But all I could do was repeat myself.

I really wondered if I was kidding myself one time. It was early evening and I was writing in the Mitchell Library. I didn't write much at home any more; Helene's mood was poisonous, and there was an oppressiveness about her I couldn't take. I'd spend the days in the flat, going over

Mike's book with him, but by the time Helene got home from work I was usually off to the library.

On this particular night I'd produced ten pages of nothing by the time the library closed at nine. I walked home wondering what'd made me think I was a writer in the first place. Suddenly, the idea of boring classes at Langside College followed by a nice steady job seemed more attractive than I can even tell you.

I only had to go home to realise how much I wanted to be a writer. Helene was sitting in the living room stolidly watching TV. There was no one else in the flat.

I made tea for us both. She smiled briefly and said thanks when I handed her a mug. We didn't talk as we drank our tea and stared at the TV for half an hour. Then I stood up and said, "I'm going out for a walk. I won't be long."

She got up to make more tea. "Why did you bother coming back here at all?"

"Don't be a kid. I just need a walk. I'll only be about an hour. I just need to think. I don't know what's up, but my writing's just not – "

She shook her head, hard. "I don't want to hear about your problems, Kevin. I'm not particularly interested in your problems. I think I might have problems of my own. I'm pregnant."

As soon as she said it I knew it was true; as soon as she'd said it she sat down in a chair with the look of a bull shot between the eyes. I knew it was true, but I still did the hoary old cliché:

"You can't be."

We'd used withdrawal with no problems for quite a while. The only time I came inside her was during her period. Then I remembered our drunken fuck at Mike's party. I came inside her then, but that was two days after her period ended, which should still be safe.

"I am," she said. "I've had a test."

"Was it one of those do-it-yourself tests? They're sometimes wrong."

"No. I did use one of those first, but then I went to the doctor's. I'm pregnant."

I put my arms around her. "What do you want to do?"

"I'm going to have the baby."

I held her and tried to think of something useful to say. After a while she told me she wanted to watch the rest of the TV programme.

I went to the bedroom and lay on the bed. I pulled the duvet up to my chin and looked out of the window. I felt lonely and guilty. Somebody was going to appear that I didn't even know.

This had nothing to do with anything I'd ever wanted, or what I wanted now. I didn't want kids. I wanted to write. I really wanted that. Now I'd had a couple of things published, and a director was interested in looking at anything I might write for the theatre, I wanted to be able to get on with it. I didn't have anything else. And now a stranger was coming along who was going to take it away.

Pregnant women are supposed to be moody. Helene was, but it was a lot easier to deal with than the way she had been. Scared as she was, she really wanted to have the kid. It gave her some focus and she was happier.

But her happiness had nothing to do with me. I was excluded. It was between her and what she was carrying inside her. I realised, I think for the first time, that men are different from women. And Helene became even more different now. Beautiful and wonderful, but different from anything I knew about. She even looked different. Everything got bigger: belly, tits, arse, and her colour changed.

She was constantly horny, but she'd never make the first move any more. She felt ugly. The sex was great, though — we had to dog-fuck and I didn't have to withdraw. But I never quite knew whether I was fucking a girlfriend, a daughter or a son.

I was as miserable as she was happy. We agreed that when the kid was born I'd have to get a job. Any job. My writing would have to fit in wherever it could.

So I went to work on a play, hoping to get it finished and sold somewhere before then. But I couldn't write as many hours a day as I once had; Mike and Helene were dividing my time between them, and not leaving much for me. Mike was plodding along with *The Book of Man*. Every day he'd want me to look at it, to suggest cuts and changes. Usually I'd suggest that he cut about half of whatever he showed me.

He was getting to devote as much of his time to his book as he wanted. In the evenings he'd write and in the afternoons he'd discuss his writing with me. I was writing for barely an hour or two a day. When I wasn't helping Mike, Helene needed attention from me all the time.

Her figure was different and she was scared. She'd look in the mirror and cry. She was never more lovely, but nothing I said to her could tell her that.

I couldn't go anywhere without her thinking I was going to leave her. Once, I'd arranged to climb a hill with Stewart Greenwood and Davy McGravy. Greenwood arranged to come and pick me up at six in the morning. Helene was awake before me. She was crying.

"What's wrong?" I asked her.

"Nothing." She went on crying.

This was a familiar scenario by now. "What are you crying for, then?"

"Nothing. You'd better get ready."

I got dressed and put on my hiking boots. My rucksack was already packed. I went to the kitchen, drank some water and had a couple of bananas for breakfast.

The door-buzzer sounded. I picked up the entryphone. "Okay. I'll be right down." I went back to the bedroom to get my jacket and rucksack. Helene was still awake. "Right. I'll see you tonight," I said.

She nodded, smiled, started to say something, stopped.

"What?" I said.

"It's stupid."

"Tell me anyway."

"Are you definitely coming back?"

I laughed. "Of course I'm coming back. D'you think I'm going to stay on the summit of Ben Lomond?"

"I know it's stupid. I'm just scared you'll go and not come back. I feel ugly. And I'm being such a pain in the arse I'm scared you'll get fed up with me and go."

I sat on the bed and hugged her. "No chance of that happening." She clung to me. The buzzer sounded again. "Look, I'll have to go. I'd just call off going, but Davy and Stewart've been looking forward to this. I couldn't do it to them."

I did it to them, though.

We were a couple of miles out of Glasgow when I told Stewart, "I'm not going."

He looked at me. Davy was dozing in the back seat. I was sitting next to Stewart in the front. "Not going where?" he said.

"To climb. To the hills. I can't go."

He saw I was serious. "How come?"

"It's a long story. I can't leave Helene. I shouldn't have come out in the first place."

Stewart sighed and nodded. He turned the car around and headed back to Glasgow.

"I'm out of order," I said. "I'm sorry." *But I love this woman.* "I didn't think I'd do this to you."

"Don't worry about it."

"Will you and Davy still go?"

"Yeah, might as well." But I knew he wasn't keen. I was his friend, Davy more of a friendly acquaintance. The climb had been planned between Stewart and me, and Davy at the last minute had said he'd like to go along as well.

I opened my rucksack and brought out the food and fruit juice I'd packed. "You can take this with you," I said. "I won't need it."

"Thanks."

"I'm really sorry about this, Stewart. But I need to go back to her."

"Don't worry about it. Go."

We drove the rest of the way back in silence. It wasn't the nicest day for a climb anyway. It wasn't cold, but there was a mean drizzle and the sky was low and packed with filthy grey clouds.

I got Stewart to drop me off in Great Western Road, about ten minutes' walk from my flat. I wanted to stretch my legs and get some air in my lungs.

McGravy woke as the car stopped and I got out. He looked around him, blinking stupidly. "Whit we daen' here?"

"You're in the Twilight Zone. We've been driving for

miles and we can't seem to get away from Great Western Road," I told him. "Go back to sleep."

"Aye. I think I will." And he did.

On the pavement, I reached into the car and hauled out my rucksack. "Have a good climb," I told Stewart.

He nodded. "Don't worry about it. Everything'll be fine." We suddenly grinned at each other, saying nothing. Then he drove away and I waved as he went.

It was still very early, but a few shops were open. I went into one of them and bought a paper and a can of coke. As I paid, I noticed there was a small display of tacky birthday cards. I bought a pink one with a picture of a kitten and the words TO A BIG GIRL WHO'S FIVE TODAY on the front. In it, I crossed out the word "birth" in "Happy Birthday" and made it "Happy Everyday".

I walked along the road and drank the coke. I was thinking about rainy hills and huge distances. All that space. I felt tight, like I wanted to cry. I walked as slowly as I could, but eventually I had to go up the stairs and into the flat. I woke Helene and gave her the card. She was glad I'd come back and she cried a little. I got into bed with her and we fucked gently and fell asleep.

Men and women worry about different things as the day of birth gets nearer. Women worry about the kid. Men worry about the woman.

I felt like a potential murderer. I was afraid Helene would die producing this stranger. I had never been religious, but now I prayed every day. The prayer was always the same – *"When I go to the hospital, please give me my girlfriend back. Please look after her."* I never once mentioned the kid.

The day he was born, it was winter in Glasgow. It was grey and beautiful in the afternoon and the huge tall trees in the West End were bare. I walked around looking at things and feeling the cold day and thinking maybe I'd done something.

I'd felt so helpless during the birth. It's supposed to be a gift, a miracle, and you're supposed to feel humble and privileged as you see it happen. All I wanted was to stop Helene from hurting. I held her hand and heard her gasp and whimper and I kept telling her it was all right and I wanted to make it all right for her and there was nothing I could do.

And later I'd held the kid and felt nothing but a desperate need to hold Helene. And when I held her she asked me if I was glad and I said yes.

And when I left the hospital I went to the West End and walked, not knowing where to go. I didn't want to go and see Mike, though I'd promised him I would. And I wasn't ready yet to go back to my flat and have to deal with flatmates who'd probably want to use it as an excuse to have a party.

I walked down Byres Road. It was dark by five o'clock. I thought about going into a café or a pub, but I was too restless and I might have met someone I knew.

I kept on walking. I'd slow down from time to time and look in shop windows. I liked the craft shops. I'd stare at a window display for a while and then walk on.

One window had a dark background and I could see my reflection. Peaked army surplus cap, big brown second-hand overcoat, pale face, glasses. I looked so young, and I started to cry.

There was music coming from one of the shops, guitar

music, a sad and introspective song. I knew some of the words, and found myself singing along, mumbling tearfully. It was a record shop, and I looked in the window for a while. For some reason I found myself looking at the picture of Don McLean on a record sleeve, looking at his face and wondering if he'd had kids too and what it'd been like for him. And as I walked back to the hospital to visit Helene and our child again, I looked at just about everybody I passed in the street and wondered about them.

When I arrived at the hospital, Mike was there and so was Moira and so were quite a few other people and everybody was talking and laughing and asking questions, sometimes asking me but mostly asking Helene, which was just as well because I didn't have any answers.

There was no real sense of neighbourhood or community around the West End. People lived too transiently, moving in and out of flats, to really get to know each other and get involved in each other's lives.

And yet, among the people who lived in our block, word had got out about Helene. It was strange; nobody really knew her, but people talked, and told each other that the cheerful blonde girl with the dark skin was in hospital having her baby, and about half a dozen good luck cards, signed with names I didn't know, came through our door.

Everybody wanted to know the day and time she got out of hospital. When the taxi stopped outside our close, neighbours were leaning out of their windows.

"Boy or girl?" someone shouted as we got out of the taxi.

"A boy," I shouted. Helene just stood there and smiled, holding David in his blue swaddling clothes. I banged the door of the taxi shut and paid the driver through the window.

"What's his name?" called Margaret, who was eighteen and at university and lived in the flat below us.

"Rasputin," I called back.

"You're kidding."

"Yeah."

"I wouldn't have put it past you to call him that."

I laughed. "His name's David."

There was a round of applause from our neighbours. We both laughed and said thanks and went upstairs to the flat.

Our flatmates had a party for us. Some friends came round to have a look at the baby. I felt like I was at someone else's party, a stranger being tolerated out of politeness.

They all left quite early, knowing Helene was tired. Then Mike arrived and showed me something I had never seen before and would never see again, something I've never got near to understanding.

He arrived about ten-thirty. "Sorry I'm so late," he said when I opened the door. "But I couldn't have faced the party. I wasn't in the mood to deal with a bunch of people."

"I wasn't either," I said.

In the hall, he stopped and looked at me. "Am I showing up at the wrong time? If you need some time to yourself, just tell me to shove off. It's no problem."

Pause. I looked at him, saw how tired he was. It was like looking in a mirror. I smiled and put an arm around his shoulders. "Nah. It's good to see you. Come on in."

In the kitchen, I made some tea. Suddenly Mike said, "Will you do me a favour?"

"Yeah. If I can."

"Can I see the baby?"

"You saw him at the hospital."

"I know. I mean I'd like to hold him."

"Serious?"

"Yeah."

"Why?"

"I just would."

"Well, he's in bed with Helene. They're asleep. I don't want to disturb them."

"Okay. It doesn't matter."

Helene called my name from the bedroom. I went through. She was still awake, lying in bed holding David. "I heard you and Mike talking," she said. "Bring him through here. I'm not sleepy, and David certainly isn't."

Mike came in and we both sat on the edge of the bed. "Is it okay if I hold him?" he asked Helene.

"Yeah. Of course." She handed David to me and I passed him to Mike.

Mike took him gently, nervously. "I'm afraid of hurting him," he said.

I laughed. "Join the club. Every time I pick him up, I'm scared I'll drop him or squeeze him or something."

Helene smiled at Mike. "You won't hurt him. Just be gentle. It's okay as long as you're gentle."

Mike held David, who looked at him with eyes out of focus, the way babies do. Then Mike started to cry.

It wasn't a quiet sniffle either. He sat there and sobbed, some of his tears falling on David's head.

"Mike," said Helene.

He shook his head and went on crying. I didn't say anything, just sat and watched him. Eventually he gave David back to Helene. "Thanks," he said. "I'm sorry about getting like this."

"It's okay," said Helene. "Are you all right?"

"Yeah. Thanks."

"D'you want to talk about what's wrong?"

"No. I'm okay." He stood up. "Right, I'm going. Enough of being pathetic for one night."

Outside in the hall, he asked me, "Can I come round tomorrow and bring some of my book for you to look at?"

"Yeah. Come round anytime after one." At the door, I hugged him and said, "Will you be okay?"

"Yeah." He laughed. "Let me go, you're making me horny." He turned and went down the stairs without saying anything else.

We never talked about that night – I wanted to, but he wouldn't – and I never figured it out. I don't know if there was some connection with him and David that I couldn't see, or if maybe it was just that nobody had been kind to him very often.

Whatever the effect David had on Mike, it was a lot longer until he had any real effect on me. Before then, the closest I got to feeling for him was when I first held him.

Somebody had told me that some religions which believe in reincarnation also believe that babies are born with full memory of their previous lives, and have perfect eyesight. This supposedly lasts for about a day. Then the memory fades and the eyes go out of focus and the baby becomes a baby as we understand it.

This all came into my mind when Helene handed David to me for the first time. I held him and looked at him and said he was beautiful, and I suppose he was because he is now, but all I felt was relief that Helene was all right.

Then I saw his eyes. Blue, perfectly focused and looking at my face. And I remembered the New Age guy I'd spoken to telling me that while the kid still has the memory and eyesight from his past incarnation, he'll copy any gesture you make.

I looked into David's eyes, grinned at him and stuck out my tongue. For two seconds he just kept looking at me. Then he smiled and his tongue came out and I almost loved him.

In the days that followed, I tried similar things with him. But he never saw me, let alone copied me.

No matter what happened later, Helene loved him back then. She loved him so much she made herself ill.

In the three months since the birth, her milk had got worse and worse. She was so into breast-feeding him that if we were out somewhere and she heard another kid – any kid – crying, she'd start to lactate.

But as the day gets longer the milk gets weaker and your kid doesn't like it so much. Helene's tits just weren't big enough and at times what she was producing must have been closer to water than milk. But she didn't want to give in and feed him with any milk but her own. And she was getting weaker and more run-down.

I wasn't helping. I'd been trying to find a job and not even getting as far as an interview most of the time, and we were broke. We were at each other's throats pretty often. We couldn't carry on living in a shared flat with a baby, so we applied for a council house. They gave us one, but we had the choice between the wasteland housing schemes on the outskirts of the city – Drumchapel and Easterhouse – and the worst area of the inner city, Possil.

We went for Possil because it was central. Since nobody

wanted to live there, we also got a better place, a fairly nice tenement flat, than we'd have got elsewhere. You could build a palace in Possil and it'd still be hard to find anyone who wanted to live in it.

When I was a kid in Maryhill, at least there was still a vague sense of safety, of community, living there with the family. Possil didn't have any of that.

Even if it wasn't safe to go out – and, believe me, it wasn't – it wouldn't have been so bad if you felt safe and secure in your flat; you could just sit with a mug of tea and watch the fights from your window. But there was never that distance. I never had the feeling that there was no chance of somebody knocking on our door – or kicking it in – and getting us involved in something.

I was more or less left alone, though. When I left the flat it was to leave the area, so I wasn't hanging around. The people I passed in the street didn't know me, and what they saw when they looked at me was a tall guy with a cropped head who never smiled. So I was seldom hassled, and what hassle I did get never went beyond the verbal.

During the day the area was just depressing. Junkies, AIDS sufferers, winos – and few of them even into middle-age. But at night there was an air of menace so thick and heavy I used to imagine our windows caving in under its pressure. Anytime one or both of us had to come home after dark, we'd get a taxi right to our close, no matter how short of money we were.

We'd sit in our living room and listen to the Possil soundtrack – screams, bangs, drunken singing – outside, and we'd feel glad our flat wasn't on the ground floor. We'd hear some woman crying for help in the street below, then a vicious chorus of male voices singing:

> She's a cow!
> She's a boot!
> She's a fuckin' pro-sti-tute!
> Na-na-na-na-na-na-na!

Calling the police wasn't on; we couldn't afford a phone. And so it went on from day to day and week to week, Helene trying to feed David and us trying to love each other through the misery of it all.

And I wasn't helping. With no job in sight, I had finished writing my play and the guy Mike had introduced me to was going to put it on. But his theatre company had no funding and so the production would be a "profit-share" – which, realistically, meant I wouldn't get any money for it at all. So most days I was in rehearsals with the actors and director working on something I'd no hope of being paid for. Helene couldn't get any work – and at that time wouldn't have left David anyway – and was depressed most of the time. It wasn't the bleakness of our situation as much as that there was no end to it that we could see.

It got so ugly between us that when I woke in the mornings I couldn't wait to get up and leave for rehearsals in the West End so I wouldn't have to talk to her. I'd come home in the early evening and feel there was something solid between her and the kid that I didn't understand.

I didn't resent his being there; I didn't feel anything for him at all. And then Helene's milk got really weak. One night she was so sick and worn-out that she had to go to bed early. She slept, but David didn't. He'd cry, she'd get up and try to feed him, he'd suck at her tit for a while, then she'd go back to sleep. It'd only be a few minutes before he'd start to cry again.

The third time it happened, Helene didn't wake. I was in the living room reading when I heard his wail. I went to the bedroom, stood over his cot and looked at him. He was crying with his mouth open wide, little face red with confusion and frustration.

I'm not sure if that was when things changed between us, or if they'd already changed and this was only the moment that I realised it. All I know is that how I felt for him was suddenly different.

I looked at him and whispered, "I'll make you sleep, kid." I picked him up and carried him through to the living room. He stopped crying as I held him, but started again when I laid him on the couch and went to the kitchenette to warm some milk. Ordinary milk, courtesy of cows.

I held him as I fed it to him. He sucked it from the bottle and I kissed him on the forehead. "Eat, eat, eat – sleep, sleep, sleep – I love you – now I can look after you."

He fell asleep in my arms. I sat there on the couch for a long time, letting his fierce trusting little body suck warmth out of me. I knew I should put him back in his cot and get round to some work I had to do, but I didn't. There were sections of the play I'd promised to revise in time for rehearsals the next day, but now it didn't seem worth letting David out of my arms for. In fact, all the plays and all the poems in the world suddenly didn't mean anything to me.

I love you, kid. And I've got you. Thank God I saved you from that stupid woman. The stupid woman who hurt you because she loved you, because she wanted to give you everything.

Now I knew what was between Helene and David. And

now I had it too. And I sat there and held him and crowed like a fucking bastard.

Mike began losing it badly. He was doing enough junk to overdose a dinosaur and he was fucking whatever he could get his hands on – male or female. I sometimes wonder whether he really enjoyed it as much as he made out, or whether he was just playing at being a decadent writer.

His book was barely moving at all, though that wasn't the way he told it. I'd go round to see him and interrupt some orgy or other and he'd greet me with, "It's all happening! It's *all* happening!"

But all that was happening was that people were shooting junk or sticking their cocks in each other. Some of Mike's new friends christened me Kev the Calvinist; and they all reckoned I'd resigned the last of any Bohemian credentials when I went and got a job.

It took me long enough to find one, but eventually one of the community newspapers – impressed by my writing – took me on as a news reporter and TV critic. It was a small freesheet, the kind that's distributed by being stuck through people's doors and funded through advertisements and local government grants. But it paid enough to make the rent and get David what he needed. Also it got me out of Helene's way.

Things had got so bad between us that we were more like cellmates in the same prison than lovers in the same house. She had no life but for David, and where he was concerned she wanted him for herself. She saw me as competition.

Not that I was around much to compete with her. I worked eight hours a day for the paper, and in the evenings

I'd be with the theatre group or at work on my own writing. Helene thought I had things that she didn't, and when I was around David she thought I was stealing a part of the one thing she did have.

I wasn't any happier than she was. My play was produced, got good reviews, got good audiences and made barely enough money to cover the cost of putting it on. My share of the profits turned out to be a free drink at the last-night party. I was asked to write another play and I said I would, but they told me I'd better not expect to make any money from that either.

The job at the newspaper was slowly making me sick. Maybe it wasn't that job particularly; maybe it was just working for someone else. It's so brutal and tiring, the way it can push you down and knock the heart out of you. It's not getting up at a certain time and arriving at a certain place at a certain time and leaving at a certain time and coming back again at a certain time – it's knowing that you have to. What's worse is that, through age or job experience or academic qualification or sheer good luck, one adult is in a position to order and insult and abuse and shout at another adult who isn't in a position to reply in kind. It makes everyone a tin god. Everyone likes having slaves to beat, as they're beaten themselves. And working on the grind wears you out. After a week of it you're so tired that you use the weekend just to catch up on your rest before going back to another week of it.

I couldn't take it. The editor's name was John McArdle, and he was one of those people who make you wonder if cancer is always a bad thing. He'd edited this same small paper for years, but he'd somehow convinced himself that he was some kind of press baron. He expected you to feel a loyalty to the paper that wasn't far from religion. Work overtime, work unsocial hours, you name it. He despised any journalist who didn't work for him and most of those who did. I was the youngest of his slaves, and he loved to patronise me.

We hated each other as much as I hated the job. But he wouldn't fire me. Without meaning to, I'd made myself indispensable; even McArdle was taken aback by the speed with which I could write news stories. I'd go to the district or sheriff courts first thing in the morning, then go to the office to write up the stories and see if any interesting press releases had come in. I'd spend the afternoons hustling after whatever news was happening locally, as well as covering council meetings, funerals, weddings and anything else that could be even vaguely seen as newsworthy. I don't think I'd be exaggerating if I said I produced more copy per week than the other two full-timers and all the freelancers put together.

So McArdle rapidly realised it wasn't in his interests to sack me. Unfortunately, he had me over a barrel; he knew I couldn't afford to quit, because the dole would say I'd made myself unemployed voluntarily, and I wouldn't get any money. In the past, I'd just have said fuck it, quit the job and survived whatever way I could. But David and Helene wouldn't see it that way.

I warned McArdle that if he didn't raise my pay and stop fucking with my head, I'd get a job elsewhere. He told me to go ahead.

I took him at his word and applied to every small paper in the Glasgow area. None of them had any jobs going, at least not for me. McArdle knew it, too.

So I tried to goad the old fucker into firing me. He was

way too wide to fall for it, but – give me credit – I got him close.

I came in one morning at eleven-thirty. I was taking off my jacket when McArdle looked at me and said, "It's half past eleven."

I sat down at my desk, picked up the phone, dialled, listened briefly, put it back down. I beamed at my master. "I think you're right," I told him with enthusiasm. "You say it's half-eleven. My watch says it's half-eleven. The clock on the wall says it's half-eleven. And I've just phoned up the speaking clock, and it says it's half-eleven. So I reckon it's probably about half-eleven."

McArdle glowered at me but held on to his temper. "You're late," he said.

I jumped to my feet and clapped my hands. "*I* bet *I* know how *you* know I'm late!" I enthused. "I bet you've figured out I'm late because it's half-eleven and I'm supposed to be here at nine! That's it, isn't it!" I slapped my forehead. "Oh God – I should've known I wouldn't get anything past you!" I buried my face in my hands and sobbed theatrically.

"Fucking funnyman," McArdle said with contempt.

I fell to my knees and grabbed him by the ankles. "Oh, forgive me, my lord! Forgive me! I'm not worthy! I'm a germ! An amoeba! Less than a worm!"

I really thought, really hoped, that McArdle was going to hit me. He definitely got close. Then he just kicked his ankles free of my grip, called me some name I couldn't make out, and walked out of the room.

I sat at my desk and went to work, feeling considerably better. Even if I couldn't get McArdle to fire me, working there was going to be a lot more tolerable if I could get away with carrying on like this.

I was wrong, though. It didn't get any better. And soon I couldn't take it anymore. And this report appeared in the paper:

Fat Bastard Convicted

John McArdle, 50, alcoholic, child-molester, Anti-Christ, mass murderer and editor of this apology for a newspaper, was convicted at Glasgow District Court of driving a heavy goods vehicle without the proper licence.

The accused pleaded not guilty, arguing that the two-ton load he was transporting was in fact his own beergut.

Jailing him for eternity, Sheriff Andy Ghandi said, "I don't care whether you're guilty or not. I just don't like you, you fat bastard."

The story was by-lined "Archibald Saddlefart". Nobody could prove it was me, but nobody had any doubt. I had sub-edited the paper that week, so if the piece had been slipped in by somebody else it should still have been spotted by me. This principle of journalistic practice was loudly explained to me by McArdle.

"You're right," I told him contritely. "I'm incompetent. You should fire me."

The fact that this was taking place in the office, in full view and earshot of everyone who worked there, didn't stop McArdle from displaying his displeasure.

"Shut your mouth, you fucking toe-rag. This is going to court. Either you wrote that shite yourself, or you got it from somebody else – but you put it in on purpose."

I smiled at him. "Prove it."

He grabbed me by the lapels of my jacket, yanked me

close to him and shoved his face so close to mine I could have touched his nose with my tongue. "I don't need to prove fuck all – "

He never got any further. His grabbing me was as much as I needed, and the position of his face in front of mine was too good to resist. I lowered my head an inch or two and butted him as hard as I could.

It opened his face, splitting the bridge of his nose in a horizontal slash. As he exhaled in shock, the blood came out in bubbles.

He sat down in a chair, covering his face with his hands. I picked up my coat and bag and looked at my fellow slaves. They were all just watching, waiting for somebody else to do something.

"That's it. I'm out of here," I told them. "Somebody better drive the boss-man to hospital. If he calls the police, don't forget to mention he grabbed me first. It was self-defence." I knew that wouldn't be a problem; as far as I knew they all liked me, and they loved McArdle as much as I did.

I walked out. Then I just walked. It was about eleven in the morning and I had no desire to go home and tell Helene what'd happened.

I hadn't had breakfast, so I decided to go up to the West End, find a café and have a late one. As I was waiting to cross Great Western Road at a traffic light, a guy came up to me.

He was in his forties, with long blond braided hair and a beard. He wore a wide-brimmed hat and carried a huge rucksack.

"Excuse me," he said in an American accent. "Can you tell me where the youth hostel is?"

"Certainly can. Just keep going up that road, then ask somebody where Woodlands Terrace is, and that's where you'll find it. You can't miss it."

"Thanks a lot." He grinned at me, white teeth shining out of a lined brown face.

As he walked away in the direction I'd sent him in, I wished I was travelling with him. I wanted to go home and pack my big rucksack with essentials, then go to the bank and withdraw the little money I had, then go someplace. Any place. Maybe Amsterdam. *Amsterdam in the cosmos.* I'd read that somewhere, I didn't know where. I didn't know where I could go. Maybe just stand on a motorway slip road and stick out my thumb and accept any lift offered, no matter where to. But that'd probably end up with me stranded in Inverness or somewhere.

I went into a café and had a huge fried breakfast, then sat with a big pot of strong coffee. I drank it till the caffeine gave me the shakes. Then I got a book – a Raymond Chandler crime novel – out of my bag and started to read. I just read all day. I didn't want to think about what I'd just done or Helene or David or anything. I was tired of changing my life, of slamming doors and walking away from things that weren't right for me. I was tired. I didn't want to have to deal with anything. I wanted just to stay in the café and drink coffee and read crime novels, nice linear stuff where everybody has a reason for doing what they do.

Eventually it was five-thirty and Helene would be expecting me home from work. I left the café and walked up to Possil. I couldn't face telling her. It would just be so wearying. A miserable chore. I decided not to tell her that night. I'd wait till the next morning, when I'd have had some rest and I'd be fresh.

She knew already. As soon as I walked into the living room, I knew that she knew.

"Where've you been?" she said suddenly. She was feeding David, holding him against her as she sat on the couch.

"Where d'you think I've been?" I countered.

"I know what happened. The police were here. They were looking for you."

"What did they say?"

"That you punched your boss."

"Not true."

"Why were they here, then?"

"It wasn't a punch. It was a head-butt."

She wanted to throw something at me, but her hands were full with David, and he wouldn't have been her first choice of missile. "You really are a prick. They had to take him to *hospital*."

"Boo-hoo."

"You really are a *prick*."

"Keep your voice down. You'll scare David." Pause. Her shaking her head. "It was self-defence. He came up to me in the office and grabbed me. What was I supposed to do? I think he'd have hit me if I hadn't hit him first."

"No wonder he grabbed you, after that article you published. He'll probably sue you."

"Let him. He can't prove it was me."

"Well, he's having you charged with assault."

"Let him. It might go to court, but I'll get away with it. I'll plead self-defence, and even if I'm found guilty I'll still get off with a fine since I've never been in trouble before."

"A fine. That'll be nice, with you out of work. That'll be fucking *brilliant*."

I didn't answer. I went to the kitchenette to make some

tea. I heard Helene in the next room, putting David to bed. Then she came into the kitchenette.

"D'you want some tea?" I asked her.

"Yeah. Please."

I poured a mugful.

"When are you going to get a grip?" she said.

"Look, I know you're pissed off. But could we forget about it for tonight and we'll talk about it tomorrow? I've just fucking had it for today. I'm really tired and I'm fed up. I just want to read a book and get some rest and not think about it."

"Oh, okay. If *you're* fed up, let's not bother. As long as *you're* fed up, let's act as if everything's fine." In spite of her best efforts, she started to cry. "Don't you understand you can't carry on like this? You're supposed to be a grown man. You can't just do what you want."

I was so tired. I took a big mouthful of tea, letting the heat scald my mouth. "It's got nothing to do with me just doing what I want. You wouldn't believe the shit I had to swallow from that wanker."

"That's what I'm talking about. You can't just do that. Sometimes you *have* to swallow some shit."

"I wish I could. Seriously, I'm not kidding. I've heard shit's an acquired taste. I wish I could fucking acquire it. I could make money and everybody would get off my back." She just kept shaking her head and not saying anything. "It'd be lovely. Life would be fucking wonderful if I could only gobble down big beautiful dollops of yummy shit."

"Shut up," said Helene, but nothing short of a bullet would shut me up now.

"Maybe if I didn't think of it as shit. Shit's such a gross word. Maybe *merde*. That's the French. Sounds quite nice.

Quite elegant. But I'll bet it still tastes like shit. *Mummy, there's something wrong with my merde. It tastes like shit."*

She started to cry harder, really losing it. "You fucking stupid prick." She turned and walked out.

I followed her to the bedroom. "All right. I'm being an arsehole. I'm sorry." She didn't answer. "But you're not getting it. I'm not a rebel. I'm not some heroic proletarian turning on the evil oppressor. I don't *choose* not to take people's shit. I just can't. I'm not able to do it. Do you understand that?"

She kept on crying.

"Listen," I said. "When I was at school, I couldn't swallow the shit the teachers kept trying to feed me. They kept telling me I'd better start behaving myself. They didn't realise I'm *not capable* of behaving myself."

The Procurator Fiscal decided not to go ahead with assault charges. McArdle decided not to try to sue me over the spoof article. He knew he couldn't prove it and besides I didn't have any money he could sue me for. He sent me a letter saying I was dismissed from the paper for misconduct. Whether I resigned or was fired depends on how you look at it; McArdle reckoned he'd fired me for hitting him, I reckon I resigned by hitting him. O relativity.

I went to the dole and signed on. Because I'd been fired they cut some of my benefit, but they couldn't really cut that much of it because of David.

But it didn't make life easier.

Thirteen

Idiots make a virtue of suffering.

from *The Book of Man* by Michael Illingworth

SO MANY YEARS later, and the paper still existed and so did McArdle. I arranged to meet an old friend of Mike's near the street where the office was. He obviously had second thoughts about talking to me, because he didn't show up.

I went ahead and had lunch in the café where I'd arranged to meet him. It was the same café I sat in all day after the incident with McArdle, which got me thinking about him.

I walked over to where the paper used to be. It was still there, according to the brass nameplate by the front door. The same nameplate I remembered from when I'd worked there.

I was wondering what the current editor was like when McArdle pushed the door open and came out. He'd lost some weight, but I still recognised him right away.

He didn't seem to recognise me. He walked past me to his car, which was parked near the building's entrance. I looked at him as he unlocked the car door. He still had an obvious scar across the bridge of his nose. If he saw me watching him he didn't show it. He got in the car, sat there for a moment while he lit a cigarette, then started the engine and drove away.

I walked about and wondered what to do with the rest of the day.

Neither Helene nor I could get any work. That didn't make us any different from most of the people where we lived. But I could feel the place closing in and crushing us.

Possil — and other areas like it, in other cities — has been in that state for so long that it now gives birth to itself. No chance of revolution now — the anger is muted and turned inwards. Possil picks at its own sores. When somebody manages to get a new car, somebody else is bound to torch it. But it doesn't occur to them to head out to Bearsden or Newton Mearns, the places where the Nobs live, and torch a few Mercs or Rolls Royces. They don't do it to the people whose opinion matters. They only do it to each other. And who in Newton Mearns cares if a bunch of schemies on the other side of town burn their own property? And so Possil, and Maryhill, and Easterhouse, and Drumchapel all stay the same.

I was no use to Helene or myself. I wasn't writing anything. I spent most of the time in the flat now, and between the two of us we just about managed to look after David. Helene felt even worse than I did. We could spend a whole day in the same room and not speak to each other. And her misery was infectious. In the way that some people are so vibrant, so alive, that it's impossible not to be the same while you're with them, Helene could drain any positive energy you might have. She would sit there, hardly moving or saying anything, just her hurt shining blackly out of her, and make the room seem grey and dimly lit. I began to think of her as the Black Hole; as black holes suck in matter, I could feel Helene's presence sucking away my freedom, my joy in trivial things, the small optimisms I managed to muster.

One of our neighbours was kind to her. A woman of about fifty, she'd lived in Possil all her life. She was small and brown, with a twisted body and a hump on her back. Her mother had been white, her father West Indian. When she was a baby, her mother had given her to some local kids to play with. Because of her colour – this was the 1930s – they'd regarded her as a toy rather than a real baby. So one time when they were playing they dropped her on the pavement and her back was damaged so badly that this hump developed.

But she was friendly and generous, which surprised me at the time but doesn't now. I wish I could remember the woman's name. That seems important somehow, maybe only because she's probably dead by now. I don't think Helene would have managed without her. The woman would go shopping for her, or they'd go together. More importantly, the woman would take David for a few hours whenever Helene couldn't handle it.

I was hardly there. *Thus Spake Andy Schuster* had come out, and Mike had invited me to read at its launch, as a sort of opening act for him. Then the Edinburgh Festival came round, and we went to Edinburgh and crashed on floors and couches and read at different venues almost every night for the entire three weeks. I sent Helene a few cards, but there was no phone to call her on and, if I'm honest, I think I preferred it that way.

Nothing had changed when I got back to Possil. I knew I

loved Helene, and loving her in the state I was in was like wanting to fuck someone and not having any genitals. I wasn't real to her, and she'd gone so far away I wasn't sure if I could really see her.

I lost it. I don't know exactly when or how it started, the exact border between being miserable and being crazy, and when I crossed it. But I crossed it all right.

It was a quiet, undramatic sort of craziness. I attached a strange significance to the placing of objects. For instance, if something good happened on a particular day – say a cheque arrived for a poem I'd had published, or Helene was a bit warmer towards me than usual – and on that same day the bedroom curtains hadn't been opened, I'd try to leave them closed every day after that, for fear that things would get worse if I opened them. It got to be more than superstition – I observed these habits with a religious obsessiveness. I would make ridiculous excuses not to open the curtains, to leave the frying pan on the cooker whether it was being used or not, to keep a newspaper for weeks after it was out of date because Helene had been in a good mood on the day we'd bought it.

It's surprising how easy it is to lose your mind without anybody else knowing anything about it. Helene had no idea. Neither did Mike – although he was moving so far into a strange place in his own head that he probably wouldn't have noticed anything wrong if I'd shown up at his place wearing a Superman outfit, talking like Bugs Bunny and telling him about my astral conversations with Rolf Harris.

My actual behaviour really wasn't much less crazy than that, only less obvious. I carried on getting up each day and eating and shopping and vacuuming and doing readings and helping Mike with his new book. And I went quietly off my rocker and nobody noticed.

Nobody seemed to wonder why I always wore the same clothes, or to wonder how these clothes managed to stay clean. They didn't know that once or twice a week I'd take these clothes off, uneasily put on other clothes and then head for the nearest launderette. I'd wash and dry the clothes I'd just taken off, then go straight home and change into them right away.

Helene did remark, "You seem to like that shirt and jumper."

"Yeah," I said. "I do. I don't feel like I'm me without them."

She just smiled. I wonder if she'd have smiled if she'd realised it wasn't just the shirt and jumper – it was also the jeans, socks and underwear. It was the shoes too, but that wasn't a problem; I only had the one pair.

I think there might be people who spend their whole adult lives doing this sort of thing and covering it up. If that'd been my only problem, I might still be at it.

But I got sicker. Maybe everybody does. I was trying to ignore something inside me, and it wasn't about to be ignored. I began to get pain in my stomach; sudden, cramping spasms that would last for a few minutes and disappear. Then it took longer to disappear. And after a while it didn't disappear at all.

I lay on the living room couch, huddled in sweating pain, while Helene went out and called a doctor. It took nearly two hours for him to arrive. In that time, I hurt so much I cried like a child. It was like having toothache in the stomach. Helene tried to help, bringing me cups of tea, hugging me and stroking my hair. But that made it worse;

when you're in that kind of pain you don't want to be touched. You just want to be left alone to lie quietly and nurse yourself. Like a wounded animal, I wanted to lash out at Helene, get her away from me. But I didn't tell her. She was already so far away, I didn't want to distance her any further. So I lay in her arms and sweated and cried and waited for the doctor.

When he arrived, he checked me over and said there was nothing seriously wrong with me. "You don't have a serious abdomen," he told me.

"Well, what kind of abdomen have I got? A frivolous one?"

"There's no swelling. It'll just be gastroenteritis."

"What's that?"

"A bug in your gut." He gave me some painkillers and told me to rest. The pain would eventually go away by itself.

It didn't. It got much worse. A few hours after the doctor's visit I was actually screaming in pain. Helene called an ambulance.

The pain suddenly disappeared when they got me to the Western Infirmary. A doctor examined me, feeling my abdomen in exactly the same way I'd been examined earlier.

He said there was nothing wrong. I insisted there was. They spent the next few hours doing tests on me. At some point I stopped talking. I just did as I was told: lay down, sat up, got on the trolley, got off the trolley (in more ways than one), took my gown off, put my gown back on.

At about five in the morning a doctor came and talked to me. "There's nothing wrong with you, Mr . . . Previn."

I said nothing.

"There's nothing wrong with you *physically*. But you seem to be pretty distressed."

I still didn't say anything.

"I don't think it'd be a good idea for you to go home right now. What do you think?"

I said nothing.

"I've talked to Helene and she agrees with me that it'd probably be better if you stayed in hospital until you feel a bit better." Pause. "What do you think? It's entirely up to you."

I made a huge effort and shrugged.

So I stayed in hospital. Not that hospital, though. Not the Western Infirmary. I thought they'd probably send me to Gartnavel Royal, the mental hospital out Knightswood way. But I was taken to Stobhill, far out of town, where they had a psycho ward.

Ward 24B, I remember. At least, that was the men's unit. The women were kept in ward 24A, and the sounds of suffering I heard coming out of there made me grateful I was born with a cock.

Not that 24B was Happy Valley. And not that I really had any choice about being there, no matter what the doctor had said. I was a voluntary in-patient; all the inmates were. But the joke is this: if you wanted to *stay* voluntary, you had to do as you were told.

The shrink in charge was called Patrick Fox. And I swear to God he was more fucked in the head than any of the patients. He was nicknamed Sparks, because of his fondness for ECT.

Electro-convulsive therapy; ECT to those who know and love it. Good old-fashioned electric shock treatment. They take depressed patients and try to cheer them up by knocking them out, applying electrodes to their temples and giving them a blast of electricity. It chases the blues away, I can tell you. Yo ho ho. Come on doc, give me a shock.

Of course, it's voluntary as well. We don't live in the Dark Ages any more. You have to agree to be given it. You have to sign a form giving your consent. One guy on the ward thought he was signing a good luck card for a nurse who was leaving.

I was crazy but I wasn't stupid; I refused my consent. So they hauled me in for a chat with the head boy, Doc Fox himself.

He was in his forties, with thick black hair, Elvis Costello specs and a singles bar moustache. "Hello, Kevin. How're you feeling?"

"Ecstatic," I told him.

"Sit down," he said. I did. He waited a while, then said, "You're refusing to have ECT."

"Yeah."

"Why?"

"Don't fancy it."

"Kevin, don't you realise you're very depressed?"

"Oh, yeah. I'll bet that's why I feel miserable."

He smiled. "At least you've a sense of humour. That's good. You didn't have it when you arrived here." That had been a month ago. "Have you been taking your medication?"

"Yeah. Of course." I'd taken it for the first few days. Since then, I'd been flushing it down the toilet. Being turned into a zombie didn't make me feel any better.

"Has it helped you?"

"I don't know. Maybe."

He changed tack. "Are you still refusing to have visitors?"

"Yeah."

"Why?"

"I don't want to see anybody. I don't want to talk to anybody."

"Not even your wife?"

"No." Then I added, "She's not my wife. We're not married."

"Oh. Your partner, then. Why don't you want to see her?"

"I just don't. I don't want to talk to anybody."

"You're talking to me."

All at once I was so tired. It was an effort just to listen to what he said, let alone respond to it. "You sent for me. I didn't have any choice. I've got a choice about having ECT."

He nodded. "Yes. Technically."

"What d'you mean, technically?"

"You're a voluntary patient. But a patient can be sectioned if we deem it necessary."

I'd heard enough gossip on the psycho ward to know what he meant: you can be detained against your will under Section 23 of the Mental Health Act.

Fox smiled at me. "I only need the signatures of two other psychiatrists. I can arrange for them to visit today."

I'd been struggling to focus, to keep my mind on what he was saying. Now I had no problem.

"Are you threatening me?"

He laughed kindly. "Don't be silly, Kevin. I'm just advising you to give your consent to have ECT. Just advising that it'd be in your best interests."

"You sad cunt," I said.

"Calm down."

"What's your problem? Won't your wife do it with you any more?"

"Kevin. You need to calm down."

"Yeah. And you need a blow job. Do you play with yourself when you think about doing this to people?"

"This is ridiculous."

"I couldn't agree more. You've just said I'm better than when I came in here. Now you're threatening to certify me and force me to have ECT!"

"No one's threatening you with anything. I simply advised you that it wouldn't be in your best interests to refuse to have ECT."

"Why not?" I stood up.

"I've already told you why not. Now you'd better sit back down. You're getting agitated."

"*Yes, I'm fucking agitated* – " I leaned over the desk at him.

Fox wasn't intimidated. He'd heard a lot worse, probably from patients bigger and crazier than me. "You're becoming hysterical, Kevin. You'd better sit down. Or I'll have to call a nurse."

Sitting down and keeping hold of my temper was harder than breaking his jaw would have been. "All right," I said. "I'm sitting down. I'm calm. What now?"

He shook his head. "You're not calm at all. There's no point in us talking while you're feeling like this."

"I'm feeling fucking wonderful. I'm about to start turning cartwheels – "

"So I think you should go to Occupational Therapy – "

"If you want me to weave baskets you can pay me the going rate."

"Or just go to the dayroom and think about what I've said."

There was a pen in the breast pocket of his jacket. I

wanted to go for it, grab it and stick it into each of his eyes.

But that would've been a sure way to a Section 23. Nice sane people don't poke their shrink's eyes out. So I got up and walked out of his office, him giving me that beaming, condescending smile, the smile you give to children when they get angry because you won't let them play with fire.

Uncle Sparks.

I went and sat in the dayroom. It was a depressing place, if I hadn't been depressed already. It was just a big room, scattered with chairs and with a TV set on a stand. But it was like a gas chamber. Am I the only non-smoker ever to have had a breakdown? In the evenings the air was thick enough to hurt your eyes.

Quite a few of the inmates suffered from depression, but we were an equal opportunity psycho ward – there were some paranoid schizophrenics, and one or two whose diagnosis I didn't know and who were just too barking mad to talk about it.

Tommy, for instance. Ambassador for Nightmare Alley. If we'd had a union, he'd have been our shop steward. It seems he was able to speak when he was admitted three years before I arrived, but he soon lost that faculty. Now he just made gobbling noises. He could walk, but he preferred to crawl about on his hands and knees.

He was in his sixties. I got his story from Malc, a tall, thin, young manic depressive who'd been in and out of hospital since he was in his teens. He told me that Tommy had fought in Africa during the Second World War. He'd been in command of a tank. During some skirmish, somebody somehow managed to get a hand-grenade into the tank. How he came out of it alive and without losing any limbs I can't tell you. He wasn't even all that badly scarred. The two guys who were with him in the tank were both killed, so maybe they protected him from the blast. Assuming Malc's story to be true, which I've always felt sure it was.

Tommy'd returned from the war, got married and lived something like a normal life. Then, more than thirty years later, the grenade's blast hit him.

It was Christmas and he and his wife were watching a war film on TV. He got up and left the room. He came back a while later with his medals pinned to his chest and a trumpet in his hand. He began parading around the room and blowing the trumpet. When his wife freaked out, he saluted her. And so began the quick march to the psycho ward.

When I returned to the dayroom after my chat with Sparks, Tommy was on the floor, being subdued by two male nurses. Malc was looking on, along with several others. Live entertainment was always appreciated on the ward.

When Tommy had been sedated and taken away to be put to bed, Malc told me what had happened. Tommy, gobbling like a turkey and crawling on all fours, had gone up to one of the female nurses and begun rubbing against her leg. When she tried to push him away, he grabbed her round the waist and tried to fuck her leg, the way horny dogs sometimes do. The male nurses came to her rescue and didn't worry too much about being gentle.

"They'll give him ECT," Malc told me.

"How come?"

"He's scared of it. And Sparks uses it as a punishment."

"Why'd Tommy sign the consent form?"

"Come on. The state Tommy's in, he'd sign consent to get his balls cut off."

"Yeah. I suppose." I hesitated. "Keep this to yourself, right?"

"Okay. What?"

"Sparks is threatening to section me if I refuse ECT."

Malc didn't look surprised. "He probably doesn't like you. The nurses think you're too cheeky."

"Boo-hoo. And I only came here to make friends." Malc smiled a little; I think that was why he liked me, because I could make him smile. "Can Sparks actually do it?" I asked him.

He nodded. "He'll do it, if he doesn't like you."

"What can I do about it?"

"Just have ECT. It doesn't hurt."

"That'll be fucking right. They'll have to catch me first. Is there anything else I can do? Sparks says he needs two other shrinks to section me. I'm feeling a lot better; surely they'll see that?"

"They'll see it, but they'll still section you. The shrinks all stick together. The only thing you can do is leave."

"What, just walk out?"

"Yeah. It's easy to section a voluntary patient. But, once you're out, it's harder for them to do it. If you leave before they can section you, they probably won't be able to bring you back."

Poor Malc. His life was lived according to the rules of the mental health system. And he'd spent so long in the system that he knew it well. I decided to take his advice and get out of there.

But others knew the system as well. Normally, it would have been easy just to leave. The place wasn't supposed to be a prison. Patients were assumed to be there of their own will, and most of them were too helpless to leave. So, if you weren't actually swinging from the rafters, the nurses didn't really keep watch on you. It would be easy to walk out and not have anybody realise until a few hours afterwards.

But not in my case. Suddenly, the nurses were watching every move I made. I could barely go off to the toilet to flush my medication down the crapper without them getting agitated. Sparks must have said something. Or maybe Malc had mentioned our conversation to someone. Or maybe Sparks had bullied him into talking. I don't know.

But I knew I wasn't going to get out of there. I was beginning to understand how it went, how they twisted things. If I tried to leave, they'd try to stop me. If I then insisted on leaving, they'd say I was hysterical. And that would make it even easier for Sparks to have me sectioned.

About a week later he called me for another pow-wow. I either signed the consent form or he signed the section. I signed the form.

ECT sorted me out. The nurses were used to being in charge, and they hadn't liked it when I hadn't taken them seriously. Since in this age of enlightenment they're no longer allowed to kick a patient's face in, the only legally allowed punishment for making a pain in the arse of yourself is the withdrawing of "privileges" – watching TV, going to occupational therapy, stuff like that. This sums up perfectly the tin-god attitudes of these people – you become mentally ill and they take charge of your life and tell you that watching TV, or something equally basic that you take for granted, is a "privilege".

Fucking outrageous.

But not being allowed to watch soap operas or weave

baskets didn't turn me into a respectful, penitent little patient. ECT did.

Malc was right; it didn't hurt. I didn't know anything about it. It's not the horror film scenario, with a slavering madman being held down by the heavies and screaming the place down as they apply the electrodes.

They gave me some dope to knock me out first. I don't know what it was, but Mike would've loved it.

It took a few minutes for me to pass out. During that time there was a feeling of being unreachable, unassailable. I felt like a fortified castle. Then I felt myself floating away, and I was happy. I thought, *Let this be it. Let this be death. If death feels like this it's all right. It's all right. Don't let me come back.*

I came back confused, with a heavy feeling in my head that wasn't quite strong enough to be called pain. I was in the dayroom. It seems I woke up in the recovery room, but I didn't remember that. I still don't.

Malc asked me how I was, and I nearly started to cry. I felt panicky, afraid of everybody. If any of the inmates had raised his voice at me, I'd have cowered away from them. It was like being a child.

An obedient child. They gave me ECT another half-dozen times during the next few months. It nearly turned me into Shirley Temple. I got more and more nervy, more and more dependent. I even wanted Sparks to like me. I'd suck up to him like a fucking teacher's pet. And when I was in the weakest, most fragile state I'd ever been in, he finally decided to discharge me.

Helene came and got me from the hospital. I was like a five-year-old being picked up by his mother. On the bus to Possil, I piteously asked her to marry me. She smiled a flat smile and said okay.

When we got home, she went into the kitchenette and took a fix.

What model parents for David we must have been – Helene out of it on junk most of the time, me almost as much of a child as he was. I hoped he was too young to realise, but it's still with him. He doesn't remember much about his mother, but he remembers her sticking a needle in her hand. That's where she'd do it, in the vein between her thumb and first finger.

Sometimes I want to tell David there was more to her than that – but then I'd have to find a way to tell him why she's not around, and it's not time yet.

Mike had told her he was getting his junk from a dealer who lived in the same street as us, and introduced her to Alfie. While I was in hospital being zapped with enough electricity to heat the homes of a hundred old age pensioners, she was in Possil getting hooked on heroin.

She wasn't yet like Mike, who needed the junk just to be more or less normal. She hadn't been on it long enough for that, and it still knocked her out of her head. After taking it, she'd just sit around for a couple of hours. I imagined it must have made her feel safe and invulnerable, the same way the dope had made me feel just before I passed out and got ECT, and in that case I couldn't really blame her for taking it.

I wasn't even all that bothered by her taking it. Not at first, anyway. Not while I was just grateful to have her around, to have her be with me and help me get through the day and not get mad at me. Not while I was being kept that way by the medication Sparks had prescribed for me and which I was still taking. And not while I was still an out-patient at the psycho ward, going for a meeting with Sparks at eleven o'clock every Tuesday morning.

Mike came by quite often. He was in better shape than he had been, by which I mean he was getting at least some writing done. He was doing an incredible amount of junk as well, but he seemed to be handling it somehow. He was also shooting plenty of speed, to keep the heroin from sending him into a stupor. He'd started seeing Paul – and got him on to junk as well – which seemed to be giving him some kind of stability.

He'd come to the hospital a few times, but I'd been refusing to see anybody. By the time I'd been beaten into obedience and was seeing anybody I was told to see, the only one still bothering to visit was Helene.

Mike would usually drop by on his way to or from Alfie's, during a shopping expedition to feed his veins. He'd come in, I'd make some tea and he and Helene would shoot up. Sometimes Paul would be with him. Mike always had a bit of *The Book of Man* with him. I'd read it and give what advice I could.

In a way I suppose I'm to blame for the weaknesses in that book, because I spotted most of them when he showed them to me. But I was too bovine to give him any strong criticism. I just told him I thought some bits were better than others and the good bits were great.

He couldn't get it together to write another continuous, full-length novel. *The Book of Man* was a series of fragments, pieces of his life. It was nothing like *Thus Spake Andy Schuster*, or anything else I'd ever read.

*

Money was practically non-existent, most of the dole going on Helene's habit. We wouldn't have been able to eat if she hadn't started shoplifting, and there were a couple of times when she got caught and we didn't eat.

I think I started getting better because of it. For months I'd been feeling nothing but fear, needing Helene to stay with me and protect me from everything.

Then I got pissed off. I don't know whether it was as sudden as it seemed, or whether it happened more gradually. I only know that one day I found myself walking around in a state just short of fury. With Helene, with shopkeepers and everybody else I had to deal with, I was impatient and bad-tempered.

I realised with a shock that I was feeling something other than fear, and I wondered how long it would last. For the next few days I tiptoed around myself, spoke to myself gently and nervously, watched myself apprehensively to see if I would cave in and cower away from what was going on around me.

I stopped taking medication. It was like waking up. I wondered how much of my docility was owing to the drugs rather than my state of mind.

I stopped going to see Sparks. I got a letter from him, expressing concern. I wrote back, telling him he could suck my sphincter. I half-expected to find myself sectioned, for the hospital heavies to come and take me away. But nothing happened.

Nothing happened. Helene took her junk, I fed David as best I could and nothing looked like changing. I asked Helene if she thought she could come off the junk.

"I don't know," she said. "But I don't want to come off it. I like it."

The junk had solved all her problems. No guilt or responsibility. She no longer felt obliged to go and visit her parents once in a while and listen to them lecture her on how she was wasting her life by being with me and how she should never have had a baby and how she should be somewhere else and how she should be doing something else and how she should be someone else.

She didn't worry about any of that any more. In the past she'd said that one of the things about me she'd first admired was that I lived my own life, rarely having anything to do with my parents, who still hadn't seen David. "I wish I could do the same," she'd said. "Just not even see them."

"Why don't you?" I'd said. "If they treat you like shit, why see them just because they're your parents?"

"Come on. My mother gave birth to me."

"So you came out of her body. So does shit. And I doubt she can tell the difference."

"I know," Helene'd said. "But they're still my mum and dad. I can't stop them from being my mum and dad."

"Why not?"

"I don't know. I wish I could."

Now she could. Now they weren't even real, weren't even an issue. I don't know how she felt about David or me. I asked Mike, and he said all she could feel would be the numbing euphoria of junk.

Sometimes Mike would fuck her and I'd watch. They didn't go to bed; they didn't even take their clothes off. Mike would just stick it into her, stick it in at the crook of her elbow, and tease her till she moaned. Then he'd press the plunger and her whole body would shudder in a junk orgasm.

He finished *The Book of Man* – rather, he realised he'd written as much as he could. He sent it to his publisher, who thought it was bizarre but decided to publish it.

This time, there was no celebration party when he heard the news. *Thus Spake Andy Schuster* was doing well in Scotland and he was beginning to take it for granted. He wasn't making much money, but he was still green enough to believe he might.

There was a launch of *The Book of Man*, at a bookshop in London. He asked me to read at it. I wasn't keen.

"I haven't been writing," I told him. "I haven't got any new stuff."

"Read old stuff, then. Come on."

"I don't know. I don't really fancy it." The truth was, I was afraid to leave David with Helene and I couldn't think of anybody else to look after him. "Get Greenwood or McGravy to do it."

"McGravy doesn't like me, and Greenwood's a fucking neurotic. It'd be like travelling with Woody Allen. I want *you* to come."

"Why?"

"Because I couldn't have done the book without you."

"I didn't do anything."

"You encouraged me and critiqued it for me. I want you to be at the launch." Suddenly I knew, from the strange tone of his voice and something stranger, something inside me, that if I didn't agree he'd start to plead.

About a week later I was on a train to London. Mike sat facing me and David sat on my lap.

We both had to go to the bog more often than most, me to clean and change David, Mike to fix up.

Other passengers looked at us, some smiling knowingly,

others glaring. I realised it was because of David. "They think we're an item," I whispered to Mike.

"Eh?"

"They think we're a couple. They think we're both faggots."

He looked at me and licked his lips. "Well, it's not too late. We could be."

I laughed. "No we couldn't." I laughed again, struck suddenly with what I was doing: Kev the concerned parent, taking his infant son to London for a poetry reading with a junkie. *Don't let the social workers find out.*

Mike and me. We were a pair, like two pieces of a jigsaw puzzle. On that journey the tired miseries and frustrations of Glasgow were forgotten – well, not forgotten, but irrelevant. It was almost like it had been when we'd first met – the easy insults, the mutual encouragement. The warmth. The only reminder of my other reality was the junk Mike had to take. And Mike taking junk didn't seem like anybody else taking junk. It was part of him, something that had always been there, not something he had got into and could get back out of if he tried hard enough.

And the day got better. The bookshop was in Woolwich, but we had four hours to spare. We went to Soho for a walk around and had dinner in a restaurant run by Hare-Krishnas. We dawdled a bit, and by the time we got a train to Woolwich and found the place, we were slightly late. But that'd given the audience time to arrive.

The place was packed. There were only about forty people there, but it was a small bookshop and they had to squeeze in. There was a table with a pile of copies of *The Book of Man* on it.

A guy from Mike's publishers stood behind the table. He

announced that Mike would be reading very soon, but first there'd be a short set from me. The audience had never heard of me, but they clapped anyway.

I still had David in my arms. There were some laughs as I handed him to Mike. I shoved through the crowd to reach the table. I was still carrying my rucksack. There were more laughs as I opened it and searched for my poems.

I read for about fifteen minutes. I didn't look at anyone but Mike, who stood at the back and nodded enthusiastically. I got a few laughs during my set but I didn't realise how well I was doing until I'd finished. The audience applauded so hard it made me jump.

I missed about half of Mike's set. The applause had frightened David and he was crying. It sounded like two cats fighting. I took him from Mike and went outside.

It was chilly and the street was empty except for some cars. The bookshop was one of only two shops – the other was a grocer's. All the other buildings were terraced houses. There were lights on in most of the windows. In a ground-floor living room an old man was sitting in an armchair, reading a book. I cuddled David and tried to think about being in this place and the place I'd come from and what I was doing and what I ought to be doing. I felt like I was in fragments, scattered everywhere. David stopped crying. I kissed his forehead and we went back into the shop.

Mike was finishing off. He'd been going down well. The audience seemed to respond even to the wanky, adolescent pieces. The better parts just blew their heads off. When he'd finished reading he got a standing ovation. Then there was a discussion that would probably have gone on all night if the bookshop hadn't closed. I missed most of it because David had started to cry again and I'd taken him outside.

I was still outside when the shop started to empty. Mike came out, his face flushed with excitement. "There's a party somewhere," he said. "My editor's giving us a lift."

I wasn't happy. "I can't take David to a party." We were supposed to be staying with the brother of the guy who owned the bookshop.

"Come on. It's not even ten o'clock. We don't have to stay late. But I'm totally fucking wired. If I don't go and do something now I'll be awake all night."

It was his night. I couldn't come on like his grandmother. "Okay."

I don't recall whereabouts the party was. I wasn't sure even at the time and, as these things happen, I never knew whose party it was. By the time I got there, David was asleep. Luckily, the party was still in the early stages where people are talking and the music isn't too loud.

Most of the people who'd been at the reading seemed to have found their way along. Most of them wanted to talk to Mike. I just stood nearby, trying not to look too out of place with a sleeping baby in my arms.

Then David woke up crying. I checked his diaper and realised he needed changing. I was standing in the queue for the bathroom when someone said, "Can I give you a hand?"

It was a thin, elfin-faced woman of about thirty. She wore black leggings and a skimpy black top. Her blonde hair was cut short under a leather beret. She looked pretty dykey and vaguely familiar.

"Thanks," I said. "I can manage, but if there's no table to put him on, it'll be a help if you can hold him for me."

"No problem." She smiled. "I'm Francine."

I held out a hand that smelled of baby-piss. "Kevin."

"I know. I was at the reading. Is your surname really Previn?" Her accent was Antipodean.

"It is now."

She laughed. "Okay."

"Are you Australian?"

"No. New Zealand."

We got into the bathroom. Francine held David and whispered comforting things to him while I cleaned and changed him. He quietened and went back to sleep right away.

Luckily, there was a bin in the bathroom. I rolled up the smelly diaper and put it there.

We went back to the party, David sleeping heavily against my chest.

"Can I hold him?" asked Francine.

It seemed like the least I could do. "Try not to wake him up."

"Don't worry." She took him from me. He didn't wake.

"Have you got kids yourself?" I asked her.

"No. I wish I did." From the way she cuddled David I could see that she meant it. "So what're you doing at a reading in London with a baby?"

I laughed. "I didn't trust anybody else with him, so I brought him with me."

"Mmm. I'm honoured, then."

We had a drink and talked for a while. She told me she ran an independent TV production company. That was why she looked familiar; her company had made a documentary series which she had presented.

The party got rowdier. I said I'd better go. I left her holding David while I went to look for Mike.

He'd found some kindred spirits. He was in a bedroom

with about four or five other people and they were all shooting up. I felt too awkward to ask if we could go. I looked at them all and thought, *This is what I live with. And where do I fit into it?*

I went back to Francine. "It's a shooting gallery in there."

She nodded. "I thought it might be. What're you going to do?"

I shrugged. "I'll have to wait for him. I don't even know where we're supposed to be staying."

"You can stay with me if you like."

She had a flat near Clapham Junction. It took about twenty minutes in her car, and David slept all the way. As she unlocked the door she said, "Be quiet as we go in. My husband might be asleep. He sometimes goes to bed early."

I looked at her. "You're married?"

"Yeah."

"I thought – "

She looked surprised. "You thought I was going to sleep with you?"

"No, I thought you were – "

"A dyke?"

"Yeah."

She smiled. "I am."

The flat was quiet and dark. "Yeah," she said, "Peter's asleep."

I followed her into the living room, a big uncarpeted room with spot lighting and varnished floors. I settled David down on a couch by the bay window. Francine left the room and came back with a pot of coffee. We talked quietly, afraid of disturbing David.

"I don't mean to be nosey – "

"Yes you do." She laughed. "It's all right. I married Peter

eight years ago so I could stay in the country. He's gay too. We've been together ever since. It *is* a sort of marriage. We're soul mates. We love each other, but we're the wrong sex for each other. But the sex is the only thing we don't share."

"Oh."

"Are you gay or bi?" she asked me.

"No. I'm straight."

"Oh. I just wondered because Illingworth seems to be. Judging from his writing, anyway."

"Yeah. He bends both ways."

"That's what I thought. I just thought you might be, since you were with him."

I laughed. "You're not the first. On the train down from Glasgow people thought we were a gay nuclear family – me and Mike and David."

"It happens. Peter and I really want kids, but they won't let us adopt."

"How come?"

"The official story is that there aren't any suitable kids available. The truth is they know we're gay, even though they haven't asked us and we haven't told them."

"How do they know?"

"It's common knowledge amongst people in TV. And word gets out. Also, Peter's as camp as knickers, which doesn't help."

"So what'll you do?"

"I don't know. I suggested we do it ourselves. I could do it with him, though I wouldn't enjoy it. But he says the thought of having sex with a woman grosses him out." She paused. "I'm getting broodier and broodier. I really enjoyed helping you with David tonight."

"I'm glad you were around."

"Me too."

We sat and talked until four in the morning. I found myself telling her about Helene, my time in hospital, the whole funfest. I realised with a shock that I hadn't been able to really talk to anyone since the start of my friendship with Mike.

At last Francine stood up. "I'd like to carry this on, but I've got to be up in a few hours. It's been great, though. I haven't had a talk like this in a long time."

I was to sleep on the couch. She brought me a duvet and pillows. "Will you be warm enough?" she asked me.

"Yeah, I'll be fine."

She gave me a hug of surprising fierceness, then kissed me lightly on the cheek. "Goodnight."

She left the room. I took off my jeans and jumper and snuggled next to David on the couch. Although the couch was in the lee of the bay window, there was no sound from the street outside, not even a car passing. I fell asleep quickly and started to dream.

The place I was in was the middle of a desert, and at the same time an ordinary room with a carpeted floor. I was dying of thirst and hunger.

The birds were white; they were gulls, not vultures. But they circled like vultures, waiting for me to die. There was a lot of them.

I lay down on the floor and played dead. I could feel the sun scorching me, drying me out like a raisin, even though there was no sun.

I felt the gulls getting lower, nearer. I didn't really feel it, just sensed it. Just knew. Then I could hear wings beating just above me. I didn't move.

Something pecked at my chest, lightly prodded me. I opened my eyes a little. One gull, hovering over me, luminous black eyes staring into mine.

I closed my eyes again after I'd grabbed it by the neck, squeezed my eyes shut as I squeezed the bird's throat. I heard it scream and felt it clawing my face. I was lying on my back. I straightened my arms, held it away, but it still managed to reach my face with its claws.

I got up on my knees, pushing the gull to the ground. I opened my eyes. The gull's body was jerking like it was having a fit, and it'd shit all over itself. Feathers flew everywhere.

I squeezed as hard as I could. My fingertips were disappearing into the dents they were making in its throat. I went on squeezing. I squeezed and squeezed, till the joints in my fingers ached. The gull kept struggling, then suddenly stopped.

I let go of it. I had to pull my fingers out of its throat. I could see the deep dents they'd left on the white feathers. I looked at the corpse and wondered how to eat it and drink its fluids.

Then I was surrounded by other gulls, some hovering in the air at head level, others on the carpeted desert floor. They looked at me with disgust, and spoke in human voices.

"What did you do that for?" one of them said. "What did you kill him for?"

I felt ashamed and scared. "I'm hungry – " I tried to explain.

"Oh, *right*," another gull jibed at me. "You were *hungry*. That's all right, then. You can kill who you like as long as you're *hungry*."

I couldn't meet their black, accusing eyes and I waited for them to do something to me and they didn't and that made it even worse. And when I woke up it was still dark and I didn't feel any better and I cuddled David and whispered that I was sorry.

I looked at my watch. I'd slept for less than an hour, and I didn't manage to sleep again. I lay there with David and thought about what I was taking him back to.

My mouth was dry and sour-tasting. I got up and dressed and went to find the kitchen. I made some tea and took it back to the living room. David didn't stir. I wanted to hold him again but I was afraid he might wake.

I got a book out of my rucksack and read by the light of the street-lamps through the window. I thought reading might make me relax and become sleepy again but it didn't. I finished my tea and went back to the kitchen and made more. It began to get light outside, and I heard voices and cars starting. David woke up hungry just before seven. I was feeding him in the kitchen when Francine came in wearing fleecy pajamas.

"Oh, you're up," she said. Her face was red and puffy with tiredness.

"Yeah. This one wakes early. I thought I'd better feed him in here. Didn't want him dribbling all over the living room."

She laughed. "Want some coffee?"

"Yeah, please."

She made it and sat down at the table. "Did you sleep all right?"

"Hardly at all." I took a big gulp of coffee. It was good. "I was just thinking about some of the things I told you about."

"Oh. Reach any conclusions?"

"I'm not sure. I think I did, but I'm still not sure what."

She smiled. "You'll be all right. Listen, I have to get going. What time's your train?"

"Ten o'clock."

"Well, hang out here for as long as you like. Help yourself to some breakfast. I woke Peter and told him you're here, but I don't think you'll see him. He's working tonight, so it'll probably be the middle of the afternoon before he gets up."

"What's he do?"

"He's an actor." She stood up. "Back in a minute." Ten minutes later she was back, dressed and made up. "Right, I've got to move. I'm chairing this discussion on ITV."

"About what?"

"Basically, these two scientists who hate each other's guts are coming to slag each other off, and I've got to referee it."

"When's it being shown?"

"Tomorrow afternoon. Right, I'm off. Here's my card. Keep in touch." She bent and kissed the top of David's head. Then she hugged me. "You'll be all right," she told me again.

Mike didn't make the train. I imagined him still in somebody's bed, sleeping it all off. I wasn't sorry. I didn't feel like talking to anybody. I'd left Francine's place just after she did, so I wouldn't have to talk to her husband if he did happen to get up. It took me an hour to find my way to King's Cross Station, which left nearly two hours before my train was due. I walked around a bit, bought a paper and some chocolate, and got back to the station half an hour before the train left.

I stood at the platform entrance waiting for Mike. When I realised he wasn't coming, I gratefully got on the train and found my seat. I felt exhausted but I don't think I could have slept even if circumstances had allowed me to try.

For the first hour, David was demanding and I was manic. He filled his diaper with shit and then bawled the place down. I saw my fellow travellers looking at me with the special hatred commuters reserve for the progenitors of screaming infants. I could feel psychic daggers sinking into my back as I carried David to the toilet.

"How do you manage this?" I asked as I cleaned and changed him. "How do you manage to produce so much shit? I mean, look at the size of you. *I* can't shit as much as that. If you've got so much shit in there, where do you keep your organs? You're defying the laws of medical science, are you aware of that?"

He'd stopped crying and was smiling and making noises. I finished changing him. "Okay, let's go and piss off the passengers some more."

I went back to my seat. I thought about putting David in the seat that should have been occupied by Mike, then realised I preferred to have him on my lap. He didn't seem to mind. He didn't sleep at all during the four hours the journey took, but he didn't fret much either. He smiled and rambled to himself in babyspeak, or looked out of the window with me. I wondered how much he could see and how much sense he could make of it.

We passed a bridge in the middle of nowhere. There didn't seem to be a town for miles around, just the sea on

the right of the train and miles of green on the left, with a
river running through it and this road bridge over the river.
I couldn't imagine what anybody would be doing this far
out, but there was some graffiti chalked or painted in white
on the side of the bridge. Huge capitals proclaimed:

> JESUS WAS GOD IN
> THE FLESH

and, in smaller letters under it:

> MAY ALL WHO READ THIS
> GET A LIFT RIGHT AWAY

I tried to figure it out. Maybe a hitch-hiker'd had a
quarrel with the guy behind the wheel and been dumped in
this remote spot. I imagined it, a guy standing at the bridge
in the afternoon and no cars coming, him getting more and
more uneasy as the light began to fade. Maybe he was still
there when there was no light left and all he was aware of
was the cold and maybe the rain and the occasional train
passing and all the noises you hear at night in the back of
beyond. I imagined him writing that scripture and then
later, when he'd been waiting for a long time, adding the
blessing under it, words of comfort for anybody else who
found themselves in the same unlucky place and position,
words to tell them they weren't alone. I thought of the guy
who could write that – what kind of acrobat must he have
been to be able to get such large and legible letters on the
side of a bridge? And why would he be carrying paint (I was
sure it was paint) around with him anyway? I imagined a
guy who thought fondly of other people while freezing and

wet and alone. As the train left that miserable spot to itself, I thought of the guy and wished him good things.

It was early afternoon when I got off at Glasgow Central. I didn't go home right away. I walked around some of the stores and bookshops in town. On my way up to Possil, I stopped in at the jobcentre. The ads for training schemes outnumbered the jobs three to one.

I spoke to Mike from a call-box the next day. He apologised for what'd happened in London. "I just lost track of time," he said. "I got wasted with some people at the party."

"I know. I saw you. I looked into the room, but you were too out of it for it to be worth talking to you."

"I'm sorry. Anyway, I hear you left with Francine Harrower."

"Yeah. I stayed at her flat."

"Did you fuck her?"

"I'm with Helene."

He laughed. "Wouldn't have stopped me."

"I know."

"I've seen her on TV. She presents some crap afternoon programmes."

"Listen," I said.

"Yeah. I'm listening."

"I've got to tell you something."

"Okay. D'you want to meet up somewhere?"

"No. I've got to tell you now."

"Okay, tell me."

"Okay. I love you – "

"Great. Any chance of a fuck?"

"Shut up and listen. I'm serious." I waited to see if he would shut up. He did. "Funny thing is, if I was gay or you were female, I probably would fuck you. I really love you. You're the biggest thing that's ever been in my life."

"Are you crying?"

"Yeah. Listen. If I hadn't met you I don't think I'd ever have found my life. But if I'm going to have a life now I'll have to get away from you. I'll have to get out of this scene, this whole context."

"What do you mean by that?"

"I don't think I'll be seeing you again. I'm moving to London."

"Are you kidding? When?"

"Next week."

"You're mad. Loads of people move to London. They end up sleeping in shop doorways."

"Francine's going to put me up till I find a place."

"Christ. One night with a Londoner and you're ready to move there. You'll never get work down there."

"I'll never get work up here."

"What does Helene think?"

"She doesn't know yet. I'm going to tell her tonight."

"How are you going to get down there? You don't have the money for the fare."

"I'll find a way. Francine said she'd lend me the money if it came to it."

"And you're not fucking her?"

"Goodbye, Mike." I hung up.

I walked back to our flat. Before calling Mike I'd called Francine. She'd asked for the number of the box and called me back. We'd talked for an hour and a half.

Helene was watching TV, numb with junk. I turned the

TV off and she didn't react. "I'm leaving," I told her. "I'm moving to London next week."

"Oh," she said.

"I'm taking David with me."

She looked at me. "Please don't take him."

"I'm taking him. It's mostly because of him that I'm going. You can come as well, but you'll have to pack in the junk."

"Okay." Flat, robotic.

"I don't know how you feel about me these days, but if you want we can get married once we get there."

"Okay," she said again.

She went to see her parents, to tell them she was going. I went to see mine, for the first time in more than a year.

We had about a hundred and fifty pounds between us. I didn't want to borrow our train fare from Francine – it was enough that she was going to suffer the three of us sleeping in her living room for an indefinite period – so we got on the train without tickets. When the ticket inspector came I said my wallet had been stolen. "But my chequebook's in my rucksack. I can write you a cheque."

"That's fine. If you've got a cheque card."

"It was in my wallet. But I've got I.D." I wrote him a rubber cheque and showed him my dole card. He wrote the address on the back of the cheque. I neglected to mention that Kevin Previn Esquire was no longer a resident of 282 Killearn Street, Possilpark, Glasgow.

*

I can understand why London's regarded as such a lonely place. If you move there you have to know people, you have to have a scene to go to. Otherwise, you could live there for years and never really make any friends. You could die and nobody would notice for a long time.

We had a scene to go to. Francine and Peter were great. So was Helene. She stopped doing junk as soon as we moved there, and what she went through is more than I know about. Francine knew a fair bit about junk through various people she knew who'd been on it. She told Helene not to try reduction or maintenance.

"They give you methadone, which is useless. It's more addictive than heroin! Or they give you tems, which you're not supposed to inject. It's a jelly that you swallow. But a lot of people inject it anyway, and it goes solid inside them and they have to have their arms or legs cut off. It's all crap. The only way to come off is to come off."

Helene came off.

Francine found us somewhere to live pretty quickly. I suppose she must have wanted to get her home space back as soon as she could. She got us into a reasonable studio flat quite near her own. I signed on and, because of David, we got our rent paid by the council. Even so, the landlord kept threatening to evict us because the rent was due on the first of each month and the rent cheque never arrived until the fifteenth.

I got the odd bit of casual work washing dishes, and Helene did some temp typing. But, without the focus of a heroin habit, she was drifting again. So was I, for a while, which gave us a sort of togetherness. Then, during a period when she had some temp work and I was staying at home to look after David, I started writing another play. When she got home that night I made the mistake of telling her, and something in her, the thing that was essential and good, closed to me and never opened again.

I knew I had lost her, but we still got married about a month later. With Peter and Francine as our witnesses we went to a registry office and vowed to lock the barn door now that the horse had bolted.

She became ill, and the doctor diagnosed a cyst. It wasn't all that serious but it hurt like a motherfucker. They put her on the NHS waiting list but told her she could expect to wait a while. Then the company she was working for – a small heating outfit called Ultrahot – went bust. We had less money but she was so ill we both agreed that she shouldn't get another job. It was about the last thing we were to agree on.

I finished my play in a matter of weeks and it got done on Radio 4 – Francine pulling strings for me again. It wasn't a good play. It was about what was happening between Helene and me. And a marriage falling apart isn't drama, it's melodrama. It's soap opera, only more hysterical. I put in the things we were doing to each other, the affairs we were both having, the fights and the head-games. Like our life together, the play was a clichéd mess.

But it earned me some money. Not much, but enough to help put an end to Helene's pain. She'd talked on the phone to her sister, who lived in Greece. She was the only relative Helene was fond of, though they hadn't seen each other in fifteen years. She told Helene there was an American hospital in Athens and that she would pay for Helene to have the cyst removed if we could pay to get her over there.

We had just enough money. I told Helene to go.

She wasn't sure. "I don't like leaving David."

"He'll be fine with me. Go. There's no point in you being sick when we can have it taken care of." I paused and then, realising we were both thinking the same thing, I said it. "The break'll do us both good. Give us the chance to miss each other. You'll get to spend some time with your sister and you'll maybe feel better about things when you get back."

She agreed to go for six weeks. We had our final fight the day before she left. Our phone rang early in the morning. Helene answered it, and came back to bed in a foul temper. "That was the managing director of Ultrahot. He wants me to go in and work for them today."

"I thought they'd folded."

"They have. They've got the liquidators in today. They want me to help them sort out the accounts."

"Do you want to?"

"Of course not."

"Don't, then."

"I'll have to call them back. I said I'd think about it." She went to the phone and dialled. "Hi, Alex. It's me. Mm-hmm . . . Is there no way I can get out of it? Okay. Okay. See you then." She banged the phone down and whispered, "Fuck it."

"What's the problem?" I asked, sitting up in bed. "If you don't want to do it, don't. What'd you mean, 'Is there no way I can get out of it?' What're they going to do, come round here and drag you over to their office? If you were to be executed and the hangman told you to hang yourself, you'd probably do it so as not to offend him."

"Fuck off." She got dressed and left.

★

Next morning, we fucked for the first time in months. She had a last-minute panic attack about going. "Are you sure you'll be okay with David?"

"No, I'm going to sell him to white slavers." I kissed her. "Of course he'll be okay. Come on, let's go."

She left for the airport in a taxi. She was wearing a white polo-neck and a black jacket, with her hair winding round the side of her neck and down over her left breast like a gleaming blonde wrap. She hugged David then kissed me, slipping her tongue briefly into my mouth.

She wrote me three letters, two of them from Athens. The first one said the operation had been easy and she was fine. The second one said she was having a great time with her sister and was looking forward to being with David and me. The third one was the one I expected. It arrived eight weeks after she'd left and was postmarked Glasgow. It said:

> Dear Kevin,
> I know you will most probably have guessed by now, but I am going to stay in Greece with my sister and see if I can find some way to live.
>
> I have been back in Glasgow for a fortnight saying goodbye to my mum and dad but I didn't have the guts to face you and I couldn't bring myself to phone and lie to you either. I am really sorry, Kevin.
>
> Please forgive me not having the nerve to tell you face to face. I'm posting this on the way to the airport to return to Greece.
> I'm sorry again,
> Helene

I cried a bit. And whispered "I love you", and it was true. But my strongest feeling was relief, along with wondering what to tell David when he was old enough to want to know about his mother. I could tell him with certainty that she loved him. As to how it turned out, I could only hope he'd grow to be a better man than his father and make some sense of it for himself and then explain it to me.

A couple of days after that, I got a phone call from Mike.

"How did you get my number?" I asked him.

"From Francine Harrower. I phoned her office and asked for it. Said I was a theatre director, wanting to get you to write a play for me."

"Why?"

"I miss you," he said.

"I miss you."

"How's Helene doing? Is she still off the junk?"

"Yeah," I said. "I think so."

"Good. I wish I could get off it."

"What?"

"All that stuff I used to say to you about it, and the stuff I wrote in *The Book of Man*, it's all crap. It was all bravado. It gets to be a drag, the junk. It gets to be boring."

I didn't say anything.

His tone got lighter. "Listen, you've got to come up to Glasgow next week."

"How come?"

"Tim McGuire's organised this massive reading at the Third Eye. It'll be amazing. *Everybody's* going to be reading at it."

"Well, I won't be."

"How come?"

"Because I'm not coming up."

"No way I can talk you into it?"

"No."

"Oh, well." He hesitated. "The reason I was hoping you'd come is I've got an idea for another book. Just a vague outline. I'd like to talk it over with you, show you bits of it."

"Sorry. I'm not coming up."

"Well, how about if I came down to see you? I could come down there and talk to you about it. We could do a reading together."

"I don't think so, Mike."

"Please? With everything that's going on with me right now, I don't know if I can do anything about it if you don't help me."

I picked up a dirty T-shirt and used it to wipe the tears from my face, but I kept my voice steady. "Mike, I don't want to know. Don't call me again."

He never called me again, and as far as anybody knows he never wrote another book.

Mike, I am so sorry.

That was ten years ago. Now I'm thirty-five and I seem to have spent most of my life slamming doors, walking away from things that were no good for me, things I'd finished with, things I thought I'd finished with.

After Helene left I got it together somehow. As I limped along on the broken bones of my life, David served as a crutch. When he's a man I hope to be his friend, because I was too busy looking out for him, making sure he had a home and food to eat in it, to get close to him when he was a kid. Having him around all the time wasn't easy. I get some weird moods sometimes, and just want to be left alone. Good friends and lovers you can tell to get out of your space, but not kids. There were times when I sang him songs and told him stories just to keep from screaming at him.

But it worked out. Peter and Francine helped. They still didn't have a kid and still wanted one, and they became uncle and aunt, looking after him when I had to work or just needed out to play.

I realised I was doing all right the first Christmas after Helene'd left. I spent Christmas Eve with Francine and Peter and a few other friends, but on Christmas Day it was just David and me. I switched off the ringer on the phone and turned the volume on the answering machine right down. I sat with David beside me on the couch and watched some crap TV and drank a few cans of beer. I liked the warmth and solitude of the day. I owed the bank a fair bit of money and I'd had visits from debt collectors and my landlord often hassled about the rent being late, and so Christmas Day brought a quiet security, a knowing that everybody was busy being at home or busy being lonely and nobody was going to appear at my door and bother me. Being alone with David was pleasant because I wasn't lonely. Peter and Francine had asked me to have Christmas dinner with them and I'd said no. But I think I'd have been lonely without the invitation.

Early in the evening I decided to bake some bread, but I didn't have enough flour. There was a shop a few blocks away that was run by a Muslim family, so I reckoned they wouldn't be closed for Christmas. David was asleep. I put on a coat and went out into the frozen, empty streets and began jogging the short distance. On the way, I saw this old man begging. He couldn't have been doing much business that day. I jogged past him, then ran back and gave him a couple of notes.

The shop was open and I got my flour. As I hurried back to the flat I met the old guy again. He stopped me and asked if I had any spare change.

"I gave you some about ten minutes ago."

He looked at me. "Sorry, son." There was frozen snot on his moustache and he had nothing on under his dirty linen jacket. I nearly asked him if he'd nothing else to wear, then realised that if he had then he'd be wearing it. "Sorry," he said again. "I'm just working the streets. I don't really notice folk's faces. God bless you. Thanks a lot."

Back in the flat, I got into bed with David. He woke and smiled at me. I kissed his hot face. "I know I'm an arsehole," I told him. "But I'm yours. I promise."

He pulled at my nose.

I got more plays put on, and some poetry published here and there. I got editing work from some publishers. I wrote a proposal for a TV show, based on the one Francine'd had to do the morning after we'd first met: I proposed a series called *Frictions*, in which two public figures who couldn't stand each other would air their differences. Francine's company made the show and it sold to the network and did quite well.

And I managed to get out of enough of my debt to get a

mortgage on a rabbit hutch in Tufnell Park. I had some friends who lasted and some girlfriends who didn't. And I had David. I also had the fear of going loopy again but as far as I know I never did. Sometimes I'd get tempted to wear lucky clothes or put objects in lucky positions, but I mostly kept it in check.

Fourteen

Camus said that any rebellion that brings about your own death is necessarily selfless; as you gain nothing, you must be doing it for the good of mankind. Narrow-minded, romantic nonsense. The most common and likely reason for giving up your life is that you can't or won't tolerate its circumstances. In that way, suicide is the most extreme form of rebellion, especially if you believe in a God. And it's a completely selfish rebellion.

from *The Book of Man* by Michael Illingworth

I HAD NO MORE work to do in Glasgow. I'd interviewed all the people I had to interview. I'd made notes of my own memories of Mike, things I'd forgotten until I went back and now recalled so clearly it seemed like the present day. I had more than enough material to go back to London and write the script for the programme.

But I didn't go back to London. I was afraid. I was afraid I might be cracking up again. I was terrified I was going to find myself in the same Glasgow psycho ward where I'd been all that time ago. Yet I didn't leave.

I couldn't. I'd begun hallucinating. I kept seeing this little boy who I knew I'd seen before, maybe in dreams. And I did dream about him. Only now he'd be there when I woke up. He was always crying, always angry, his thin pasty face contorted with rage and hurt, the tears running into his mouth with its broken, uncared-for teeth. I saw him and knew him but I didn't know who he was. He looked at me from the faces of kids I passed in the street. He stood on the periphery of my vision, afraid to come any closer. But I knew he was there and he frightened me.

Afraid to go home, I walked around. I walked back up to Raeberry Street, looked at the new buildings, remembered the old, the way a healthy man remembers a debilitating illness. I walked over to Cedar Court, where I'd last lived with them. I looked at the block of flats in the middle and wondered again if they were still there.

Where I come from stays the same, even when they've knocked down the old houses with no bathrooms and built cell blocks with bathrooms, or gutted the rancid old tenements and sandblasted the outsides and put bathrooms in the insides.

It stays the same, even though the children now have baths and don't have to wait for their parents to boil a big pot of water and then pour it into a plastic basin. My sister and I used to watch my mother or my grandmother do that – they'd put the basin on the floor in the middle of the room and fill it with hot water. I remember the basin was red, and I'd take my clothes off and step into it first. I was about eight, my sister about six. I'd go first. The water would reach just past my ankles and then I'd squat down, naked, shivering in the parody of warmth that came from the tiny twin-bar electric heater. I'd squat down and try to fit into the water as much as I could of my three-and-a-half stone, four-foot caricature of a body. I'd shiver like thin white paper and I'd splash warm water over myself and get the carpet around the basin soaking wet.

Then I'd jump out and dry myself with a hand-towel. My mother would wash my hair at the sink, rinsing it with water so cold I'd cry and kick my feet and my nose would run, as my sister stepped into the water I'd just left. Later, after my sister was finished, I'd get to piss in the basin rather than go out to the toilet. She was never allowed to do that, being two years younger and being a girl. Such was the hierarchy. But, being small and a girl, there were things she was spared. Nobody was ever allowed to hit her.

I was often told that my grandmother spoilt me, because I was her favourite and she had the power. My grandmother, who would scream and shake me and break my toys when I misbehaved. She'd break my toys, but that was all she could do. And she didn't understand that I didn't need toys. She didn't understand that the park they called the Low Road was the African Jungle and the red-ash wasteground across the road was the planet Mars. She didn't understand that, and if she had she still couldn't have taken it away.

If I was her favourite, I sometimes wondered what would happen to me if I wasn't spoilt, if I wasn't her favourite and didn't have her protection. I found out when I was nearly nine.

She began acting strangely, so strangely they took her into hospital and shaved her head and opened it up. But the brain tumour had gone too far and all they could do was close her head up again and give her a wig. And nobody told her she would die before her hair could grow back, but I think she knew anyway because the night she came home my youngest sister who was only a year old was being washed in the basin and my grandmother came in and knelt down on the soaking wet carpet by the basin and put her arms around the little girl and held her tiny dripping wet body against her and cried for a long time while my mother and father and grandfather and other sister and twin brothers and I stood and looked at her.

She went back into hospital soon after. My mother took delight in telling me, again and again, "Your granny's going to die." She'd get drunk and really get into it, proclaiming it like Olivier. She'd get so into it that she'd sometimes start herself crying. But she couldn't make me cry that way. I never cried once.

I wasn't sad and I wasn't afraid.

She couldn't understand it.

My grandmother didn't marry a man but a cultural stereotype. Racism, homophobia, xenophobia, he had it all – as fine an outfit of bigotries as you could wish for.

He'd fought in the war and hated all Germans. He'd served in India and could hardly contain his disgust that in Glasgow Asians owned shops and passed him on the pavement without having to bow and step aside and call him *Sahib* like they had in the Good Old Days. He hated homosexuals and often told me, "Make sure you're a man in every sense of the word." His memory sometimes makes me feel bad about being straight; if only I was gay or bisexual, I could fuck a man and at the point of orgasm I believe I'd hear the old slug turn over in his grave, then quickly turn back again for fear I'd dig him up and shove it up his arse.

He was the one who told me, "You haven't got a granny any more. She's dead." At least he cheated my mother of the pleasure. I cheated him, too; he expected tears and saw none.

I wasn't sad and I wasn't afraid.

I went back to the game I'd been playing.

I went to a lonely place, a place so lonely nobody else could go there, and nobody else I know has ever been, a place so lonely I won't ever go again, until that time comes right at the end when I have to go there for good. I was lonelier than I'll ever be again while I'm living, but they couldn't reach me there. They couldn't get to me.

They could hurt me for sure – they kept me in a perpetual state of hurt. But they couldn't make me afraid. I was so lonely.

But I wasn't sad and I wasn't afraid.

When I swore at my father and he brandished his big belt, he thought he was beating all the contempt and all the defiance out of me. He only beat it farther in. They told me they were going to have me put in a home, but I didn't know what a home was and I wasn't afraid. They invented new cruelties, and I invented new worlds their cruelties couldn't reach.

Their cruelties couldn't reach me. They could make me cry with pain but they couldn't make me cry for real. They had to hit me to make me cry, and that was only a technical victory. They could beat me but they couldn't win, because they couldn't come to where I was. They couldn't face me in my own arena, and so their precious little cruelties couldn't reach me. They didn't matter; the bruises didn't matter; the welts on my legs didn't matter; all their insults, all their names, their jibes, all their jokes about my stupidity, my emaciated body, my big ears, didn't matter.

Because they didn't exist in my world. They weren't real to me. I lived in a world where I wasn't afraid, because their cleverest cruelties only amounted to rejection, and I was so lonely that rejection meant the same to me as the threat of murder means to a corpse.

And I stayed in that place, and I learned how to stop those who tried to reach me there. I learned about bluff and about trickery, and how you didn't have to fight much if you weren't afraid, and how to be beaten but not to lose – which was easy, the nothing I had, the nothing I was.

And I got older, and I looked at them from my lonely place. And I spat in their faces, and my contempt dissolved them.

They were gone.

And I wasn't sad and I wasn't afraid.

And a girl with red hair and cold hands looked into my lonely place and saw me there. And when she said no I just nodded. But later, when she said yes, I was sad and afraid.

I couldn't believe she'd said yes. Nobody had ever said yes before. I'd never heard yes before. But she laid me down and showed me yes; she showed me the meaning of yes, swaddled and wrapped me in yes. Waves of yes warmly bathed me.

And I wasn't sad and I wasn't afraid.

★

Later, when she changed from yes to no, I was sad but I wasn't afraid. And other people said yes or no to me – sometimes one, sometimes the other – but one as often as the other.

And I did the same.

So now I was back, walking about in empty lanes, looking at Glasgow and knowing that no one I loved lived there any more.

But the face of the little boy wouldn't leave me alone.

Fifteen

At the coldest hour of the night, when you feel like you're completely alone and no one can help you, always remember – you're right.

from *The Book of Man* by Michael Illingworth

WHEN FLOOZY TOLD me she loved me, we were both drunk. We'd been to a gig by a band she was friendly with, and rolled back to my flat in a taxi in the small hours. In bed, she said she loved me and I silenced her with a kiss. She didn't say it again.

Next day was Sunday. We got up at ten and I told her I was going to pick David up from Francine and Peter and take him to a café for breakfast. "Want to come?"

"God, I couldn't eat." She was pretty hungover. She grinned. "But yeah. I'll come."

We started walking the few blocks to Francine and Peter's. It jwas a sunny morning. "Do you remember what you said jto me last night?" I asked her. "Just after we went to bed?"

She looked at me. "Yeah. I know what you're talking about."

"Did you mean it?"

"Of course I meant it. Why else would I say it?"

"Well, I feel the same."

"What?"

"I feel the same. I love you," I said.

We stopped walking. "Are you sure?" she said.

"Yeah. I've been sure for quite a while."

"Why didn't you say so last night?"

"Because you were drunk. I didn't want to hold you to something you said that you might regret when you were sober. And I was drunk too. I didn't want us to talk about it when we were drunk."

Suddenly we were in each other's arms and we were laughing. "Listen," I said. "Let's go to the café and get some coffee, *then* go and get David."

It hadn't come easily. It wasn't a movie romance. When we met she was so battered that she didn't trust anybody. She hit me with all kinds of shit to find out how safe she was, to see if I'd hurt her in return. Sometimes I suspected she actually wanted me to.

I didn't. She began to trust me more and freak out less. I remember the last fight we had. I was in her flat and she was screaming at me. I walked out.

I was about a block away when she caught up with me. She was crying a little. "Don't go home. Come back with me."

"I'm going home. This is no use. You're looking for a threat in everything I say."

"I know. I'll stop. Just come back with me."

I did. On the way she told me, "Even when I'm being an arsehole, please don't walk away and leave me. I hate that. When I was about five, my mum used to do that. We'd be out shopping or something and she'd tell me if I didn't behave she was going to leave me. That's the cruellest thing you can say to a kid."

But the fights faded away until, nearly a year on, we were saying we loved each other and sitting over coffee in a Sunday morning café. Floozy's hangover had gone and she was hyper, rambling happily.

"Do you want kids? More kids, I mean," she said.

"Don't know. I've never really thought about it."

"I want to have a kid with you. Do you want that?"

I considered. "I'm not much of a father, but yeah. I think so."

"I think you're a brilliant father." She laughed. "You won't believe this, but I even want to marry you."

"Fine by me. I'll have to divorce Helene first, but that shouldn't take long after all this time."

She went on laughing. "I mean, it's bizarre. I hate the idea of marriage. Always have. I don't respect the church or the state, so why should I want to get married? But I want to marry you."

"Good excuse to have a party, anyway," I said.

"When did you realise you loved me?" she asked.

"A while ago. It happened gradually. I didn't just wake up one morning and say *Eureka!*"

"Well, I did. The other day. I was thinking about how much of my life I'd have without you. And I realised. If you left me, all I'd have is a signed book and the memory of the best time I've ever had."

★

A couple of months later I did a reading in Hastings. Floozy went with me. We stayed overnight and went to the beach the next day.

We didn't talk much. Floozy sat and listened to her personal stereo. I lay on the sand with my shirt, shoes and socks off and watched gulls chase each other across the blueness above.

The sun was burning my pale skin. I put my shirt on. Floozy switched off her stereo and said, "I might be going to America."

"Great. How long for?"

"For good, maybe. I've been dreading telling you. But I wasn't going to write you a letter like Helene did."

I sat up and looked at her. She was looking at the sea. Her nose was shiny with sunburn. "What's this about?"

"I'm getting nowhere in this country. Record companies aren't interested in me. I'm sick of it."

"Why would it be any easier for you in the States?"

"I can get an agent in L.A. One of the best agencies there wants to sign me if I go over." She waited for me to say something and when I didn't she said, "It's all right for you. You've got everything you want. You don't really want much."

"I want you."

"I really need to get a deal. I don't want to do anything but play music. I can't give it up, and I can't keep playing in pubs and clubs."

"When would you be going?"

"End of the year. Maybe the beginning of next year."

"Where do I fit into your plans?"

She hesitated. "I'm not sure you do."

I picked up a stone, a small pretty blue and white one. I polished it with my shirt-tail and put it in my pocket. "What about . . . everything you said?"

"I don't know," she said. "I'm sorry."

"Why'd you say these things?"

"I don't know."

I lay on my back and looked at the sky again. I imagined I was actually looking down, imagined falling into that endless blueness.

I felt scared.

We decided to finish. We didn't see each other for about six weeks. David missed her as much as I did. I phoned her and we said we'd try seeing each other as friends. We did and had a bumpy month or two of ending up in bed together and me tying myself in knots over the other men I knew she was seeing.

Then I read about Mike's death and she said she'd take care of David while I was in Glasgow.

So now she was in London with David and I was in Glasgow with the angry, lonely little boy I couldn't identify or get away from.

I gave in and did it. I went into the block of flats in Cedar Court and found the door. It seemed they were still there. The same nameplate was still on the door, a stainless steel rectangle with his name in capitals.

I walked up and down the corridor, looking at the names on the other doors. Most of them had changed. And some of them were painted green or black or red. As soon as you buy your council flat, you paint your door a different colour so everybody can see you're a homeowner.

My parents' door was still council-brown. I stood in front of it and tried to figure out what I was doing. I could sense the little boy somewhere nearby, maybe out in the stairwell, sad and afraid, waiting to find out what I'd do.

I rang the doorbell. My brother opened it. I recognised him right away, even though most of his black curly hair was gone. He didn't recognise me at all, just looked at me blankly and then said, "Well?"

"You're getting taller," I said. "Your head's starting to poke through your hair."

He realised then. "Kevin. Jesus Christ. Jesus Christ."

"Are you going to ask me in?"

He stepped back from the door. I went inside and closed it. "D'you still live here?" I asked him.

He nodded slowly. "Aye. I moved back in after he went blind."

From the living room upstairs a voice called, "Robert! Who's that at the door?" It was a voice I didn't know, an old man's voice, but I knew who it belonged to.

"It's Kevin," shouted Robert.

"Kevin who?"

"Your son Kevin," shouted Robert.

"Well, is he coming in or what?"

I followed Robert into the living room. The furniture was arranged differently than I remembered, but it was still the same stuff. An old man I wouldn't have recognised in the street sat in an armchair.

"Hi," I said. "How're you doing?"

"Awright." He stood up and extended a hand in my general direction. When Robert had said he was blind, I thought I'd misheard. But he was blind all right. He couldn't even see where I was standing.

I took the hand and shook it. "I was just in town, doing a bit of work. Thought I'd come and see you."

He sat down again, carefully. "Aye? It only took you about ten years." But his tone was mild and I realised he wasn't bothered.

I sat down opposite him. "What happened to your eyes?"

"Your mother."

"What d'you mean?"

"She threw a pot of boiling water in my face."

"Fuck. Was it deliberate?"

"I don't know. She didn't know either."

"Fuck. Where is she now?"

"That depends on your religion."

"What? She's dead?"

"Aye. Eight years."

At that point Robert, who had been standing there helplessly looking at me, asked if we wanted some tea.

"Aye. Please," said my father.

I had to get out of there. I'd been there less than five minutes, but now I just had to get out. "Listen, I haven't got much time," I told them. "I've got to get a train at ten o'clock." It was now about six. "D'you fancy coming for a drink?"

My father shrugged. "Nae money."

"I'll get it."

We went to the Woodside Inn, my father's favourite pub for twenty years through numerous name changes. It was about five minutes' brisk walk from Cedar Court, but it took us longer, the old man with his white stick, my young brother – who looked like an old man himself – holding his arm.

The pub was full of old men and old women of all ages. I got my brother a pint of lager and my father a whisky. I had a coke. My brother asked what it was and I said vodka and coke rather than have to explain why I wasn't having something stronger.

We went and sat at a table. People kept saying hello to my father and brother. I recalled a day when I was twelve or thirteen and had a job delivering papers. On this day my father said I'd have to give him the couple of pounds I'd earned, because he had no money to buy food.

"You've been drunk the past two nights," I said.

"What's that got to do with you?"

"How can you do that if you've no money?"

"I've got plenty of friends."

"Good. If they'll give you money for drink, see if they'll pay for our food."

Him taking off his leather belt. Later, me curled on the floor, crying. Him sitting on a chair, breath heavy, the belt lying in his lap like a limp prick.

He had plenty of friends. They came to the table to talk to him for a minute or so. He introduced me. Some of them said they remembered me, though I didn't remember any of them. I listened to them trade news of health problems. It seemed like everybody was either just out of hospital or waiting to go in.

My father finished his drink quickly. I got another round. "I needed that," said my father. "This morning I went and got a half-bottle from the off-sales, but when I was going up the road the plastic bag burst and the bottle got smashed. I went back to the shop and asked them to replace it, but they said the bag wasnae one of theirs and they wouldnae replace the fucking bottle."

I said nothing.

"You working, then?" asked my brother.

"Yeah."

"What as?"

"A TV researcher."

"Make much money at that?" asked my father.

"Not much," I said. I found myself hoping he'd ask me for some but he didn't.

It didn't seem real. My brother was practically in shock at my presence, my father seemed unaffected and I was trying to feel something. My mother's death, his blindness, it should have seemed so enormous and it seemed so banal. We sat in the pub and talked like there was nothing strange going on. I asked after my sister and they told me she had three kids and was living with a guy in Roystonhill. I wanted to ask my father, *Why'd you have me if you didn't want me?* But I couldn't. And even if I could, I knew he wouldn't be able to tell me anything.

I said I'd better go. My brother asked for my address. I said I was between places.

"Can you get us another drink before you go?" my father asked me.

I thought about telling him he had plenty of friends, that they could get it for him. While I was thinking about it I went and got him and my brother their drinks.

"Keep in touch," my father said.

I shook hands with him and with my brother. Then I walked out of the pub.

Rain was coming down in thick blankets. I knew I should find another pub and take shelter till it stopped, but I couldn't keep still. I could sense the little boy, crying in the rain, trying to shelter in shop doorways.

I walked. I had planned to catch a train to London that night, but instead of walking down to the Central Station I found myself heading for the West End.

The rain didn't ease at all. My jacket and jeans were soaking and heavy. My rucksack felt like it had soaked up water like a sponge. Even my sweater and shirt were wet. With every step I took, my feet squelched.

I was walking through Park Circus, which is on top of a hill overlooking Kelvingrove Park. It was nearly dark. There was nobody else around; the rain had driven everybody who could to find warm rooms and dry clothes.

On the edge of the park was a statue of a soldier on a horse. As the rain swept over him in the lonely orange streetlights, he looked like he was doggedly trying to get somewhere, riding hard against the weather. I stood and looked at him for a while, him frozen in time, forever trying to leave the place behind and reach a place ahead.

The rain stopped eventually, and the statue was just a statue. The last of the daylight was gone. I went into the park, found a bench and sat down on it, exhausted, my rucksack sinking into the mud at my feet.

I knew the little boy was somewhere nearby and he was watching me. But I was too tired, too beaten, to be afraid. If I was losing my mind, that was all right by me. I might be crazy already. I didn't care. I didn't want to think any more, I didn't want to hurt any more. I didn't want to be coming from anywhere or going anywhere. I just wanted to sit on this bench in the darkness and take slow, quiet breaths of the cold, wet air.

And then, somehow, I had stopped breathing the air in and out, and now the air was breathing *me* in and out. I sat there and heard and felt the huge, gentle breathing of the air.

Then it was me that was breathing again, but not just breathing the air. I was breathing the park, feeling it fill me, then breathing it out again. I was breathing the night sky, breathing the rain clouds and the stars they were hiding, feeling them inside me, going in and out of me. I breathed the whole city, clarity and shadow, darkness and light. I breathed all the things that had ever happened to me, good and bad, and couldn't feel any difference between them. Then it was more than just the city – I was breathing everything there was, felt it all inside me, David and Floozy in their beds in London, memories of Helene and Mike and my parents, where I'd been and where I was now. It was all like air and I was breathing it.

And then I looked to my side and there was the little boy, soaked through and crying, welts on his arms and legs. He was coming towards me slowly, taking small nervous steps, shaking with fear and rage.

I held out my arms to him and he came to me and I held him hard and warm as he cried, safe for the first time ever and he held me as I cried, safe for the first time ever.

Then we sat quiet, still holding each other. He was smiling at me. I was smiling too.

"We'll live or die with it, Kevin," I said.

*

When I left the park it was after midnight, but I knew Floozy would still be awake. I found a phone and called her.

"Are you all right?" she asked me.

"Yeah."

"Your voice sounds funny. Are you drunk?"

"No. I've been crying."

"Are you sure you're all right?"

"Yeah," I said. "I think so."

"When're you coming back?"

"Tomorrow. I've probably missed the last train tonight, but I'll get the first one in the morning."

"Good. David's been missing you." She paused. "Why were you crying?"

"No real reason."

"Did it hit you hard, going back to Glasgow after so long?"

"Turns out I've never been away."

I had missed the last train. I didn't feel like hanging around the Central Station all night, but there was a pancake place nearby in Renfield Street that was open till five in the morning. I went there and ate doughnuts and drank tea and read a book.

Mike once told me that love is only affectionate obsession. At the time I thought he was probably right, but I'm not so sure any more.

Mike was a friend of mine.

Founded in 1986, Serpent's Tail publishes the innovative and the challenging.

If you would like to receive a catalogue of our current publications please write to:

FREEPOST
Serpent's Tail
4 Blackstock Mews
LONDON N4 2BR

(No stamp necessary if your letter is posted in the United Kingdom.)